Phillipa knew she'd run into Kyle at the police station.

Yet she hadn't expected to have to work so closely with him. Almost as if she'd summoned him with her thoughts, she turned and found him standing in the doorway. His presence spurred a wave of emotions in her.

"It's good to see you, Phillipa," he said. "I couldn't believe it when I heard you were coming home."

A sudden chill formed and hung in the air. "Detective Rossi, is there something you want?"

He eyed her for a moment. "I just wanted to say hello, *Sgt. Stevenson.*"

"There's no need." She wanted him to know exactly where he stood with her. She bristled at his waltzing in, as if he hadn't wounded her so deeply he'd rendered her incapable of loving again.

When he left, Phillipa sighed in relief. She chided herself for allowing her emotions to take control... there was no room in this job for personal feelings.

Jacquelin Thomas is an award-winning, bestselling author with more than fifty-five books in print. When not writing, she is busy catching up on her reading, attending sporting events and spoiling her grandchildren. Jacquelin and her family live in North Carolina.

Books by Jacquelin Thomas

Love Inspired Cold Case

Evidence Uncovered

Harlequin Heartwarming

A Family for the Firefighter
Her Hometown Hero
Her Marine Hero
His Partnership Proposal

Visit the Author Profile page
at Harlequin.com for more titles.

COLD CASE DECEIT

JACQUELIN THOMAS

LOVE INSPIRED

INSPIRATIONAL ROMANCE

LOVE INSPIRED®
INSPIRATIONAL ROMANCE

Recycling programs for this product may not exist in your area.

ISBN-13: 978-1-335-55598-4

Cold Case Deceit

For questions and comments about the quality of this book, please contact us at CustomerService@Harlequin.com.

Love Inspired
22 Adelaide St. West, 41st Floor
Toronto, Ontario M5H 4E3, Canada
www.LoveInspired.com

Printed in U.S.A.

For nothing is secret, that shall not be made manifest;
neither any thing hid, that shall not be known
and come abroad.
—*Luke* 8:17

Prologue

2006

She held her purse close to her rapidly beating heart. Every time she heard the shrill scream of a siren seemingly close by, she glanced out the window of the Greyhound bus to see if it was being hailed or followed by a team of police cars before they could get out of Miami.

This went on for the next hour as they traveled from city to city.

Normally, whenever she traveled by bus, the ride was smooth and felt like a giant cradle, lulling her to sleep. There was usually a sense of tranquility—but this time was different.

Some passengers absorbed themselves in whatever they were reading; others slept as the bus rocked from side to side, traveling over familiar roads. She could hear a few people talking, their voices rising at certain intervals. Every now and then, there was a spark of laughter. Others, like her, seemed to be alone with their thoughts. Worries drifted into her mind, worries that she hoped would erase themselves by the time she reached her destination.

Although they were all together on this journey, she felt like an outsider. The only common thread with the other passengers was that she felt the same turns and bumps of the bus.

She willed her body to relax. But the anxiety swirling around in her stomach didn't completely evaporate until the bus pulled into Lake City, Florida.

However, when she arrived at her final destination around three fifteen the next day, the sense of dread that filled her before had vanished. It was as if she'd left it on the bus for the next passenger to contend with.

She emerged out of her blue-and-silver cocoon a new person.

One determined to forget the past.

She wanted to forget that she'd shot and killed her best friend…

Chapter One

Present Day

"The Charlotte-Mecklenburg Police Department has approximately 615 open homicide cases dating back to the early 1960s. As you're aware, each case represents a victim and their families still waiting for justice."

Phillipa Stevenson sat across from Trevor Peters, the commander of the Violent Crimes Division, legs crossed and fingers knitted together in her lap. "I believe all victims need closure. So do their families," she responded.

He nodded in agreement. "The biggest fear of families who've lost someone is that a case will be forgotten. We don't want that to happen. That's why we have a dedicated Cold Case Unit. We have a tip line and a website set up where we're asking the public for help. We've closed forty-nine cases since the unit opened in 2006. We've been looking for more avenues to reach the public."

"What about social media?" Phillipa asked. "Pictures of the victims should be posted there. We should also take advantage of television and billboards as well. LAPD has had a lot of success with them."

Peters nodded again. "We're very glad to have you with us, Sergeant Stevenson. Welcome back to Charlotte."

She smiled. "Captain Peters, I'm happy to be back in the Queen City."

"I'm sure your parents are ecstatic."

"Yes, they are."

He grinned. "I haven't seen Jacob and Bethany in about six months. I know your dad's been working on a high-profile lawsuit against some pharmaceutical company. I'm sure it's keeping him busy."

"He's been working a lot," Phillipa responded. "I'll let Dad know that you asked about him. He really misses being out on the golf course. He talks about it a lot."

They chatted for a few more minutes before Peters escorted Phillipa to her new office.

She stepped inside the midsize room, taking in the four tall bookcases cluttered with books, magazines and other periodicals on the right side. On her left was a large double window overlooking the busy street below.

Wisps of pillowy white clouds played peekaboo with the early August sun. Phillipa was looking forward to the fall when the leaves on the trees would begin changing colors. It was one of the things about Charlotte that she'd missed while living in Los Angeles.

Phillipa walked around her desk, tracing the ornate edge with her fingers. She was excited about being the new unit supervisor of the Cold Case Unit, called CCU by most everyone at the precinct. It was her passion to seek justice for the victims and help their loved ones find closure.

Her new team consisted of homicide detectives, a civilian review team with law enforcement experience and volunteers with a wide array of life experiences, much like the unit she had left in LA.

She recalled the number of open cases. Six hundred and fifteen. "It's time to get busy," Phillipa whispered as she sat down in the high-back leather chair. She'd come in the previous day to meet her team. Only one of them had given her pause.

Kyle Rossi, a homicide detective. She'd had no idea he was working with CCU when she was offered the position. Phillipa might have turned it down otherwise because of her personal and painful history with him.

Twelve years ago, she and Kyle were engaged to be married. He broke it off a week before the wedding. Her recent divorce, which represented yet another failure at love, had broken her spirit. With no family in Los Angeles, Phillipa had seized the opportunity to return to Charlotte with her soon to be eleven-year-old daughter, Raya, to be near her parents. It was a safe place to heal and rebuild her life.

She paced the floor.

Why was she so nervous? Kyle Rossi was just another employee. He was on *her* team. Phillipa had known she'd run into Kyle at the precinct, but she didn't expect that she'd have to work so closely with him. She held up her trembling hands, staring at them in wonder. Her stomach was a bundle of nervous energy.

Why am I anticipating his arrival with such strong emotions?

Phillipa didn't have an answer for herself.

Almost as if she'd summoned him with her thoughts, Phillipa turned and found Kyle standing in the doorway, his presence exacerbating the wave of emotions that was already swirling inside her. A sudden chill formed and hung in the air as their gazes met and held. Her eyes strayed to his lips. Phillipa yearned to smack that devastatingly handsome grin away.

"It's good to see you, Phillipa," he said. "I couldn't believe it when I heard that you'd accepted the position. I didn't get a chance to speak to you yesterday because I—"

"Detective Rossi, I'm extremely busy," she cut him off. Phillipa wished she'd come up with another excuse. He'd caught her doing nothing more than walking around the office. "Is there something you want?"

He eyed her for a moment, then said, "I just wanted to say hello, *Sergeant Stevenson.*"

"There's no need," Phillipa responded. She wanted Kyle to know exactly where he stood with her. She bristled at his audacity to think he could just waltz up to her as if he hadn't wounded her so deeply that he'd rendered her emotionally incapable of loving another man.

When Kyle walked away, Phillipa released a sigh of relief. She chided herself for allowing her emotions to take control during their brief exchange. There was no room in this job for her personal feelings—she had to treat Kyle as she would any other member of her team.

Phillipa didn't fail to notice that he was still a very handsome man. At thirty-three, Kyle now sported a neatly trimmed mustache and beard, and she couldn't deny that it suited him as much as his expressive brown eyes and full lips that transformed into an easy smile.

She forced her thoughts away from Kyle. It did her no good to think about him in that way.

Phillipa sat down at her desk and turned on her computer. She pulled up her calendar to schedule a series of meetings with her team.

Then she looked to see the number of cases each review team member had handled in the past six months. Phillipa knew that the review process generally took about five months. She was a hands-on supervisor and intended to read over current case files to help identify any leads that needed to be followed.

Throughout the day, Phillipa randomly selected files handled by the review team and read the detailed summaries relating to the cases. She jotted down notes or queries to discuss with the team.

Before long, her eyes traveled to the silver-framed photograph of Raya on her desk, prompting the gentle tugging of a smile. There were no words to describe her love for her daughter. She was the sunshine in Phillipa's life. Her only reason for being.

Phillipa had some apprehension about returning to Charlotte, but she thought it was best not only for her but also for Raya. Her daughter was having a hard time accepting the news of her father getting remarried. She wanted her parents to reconcile—something that was never going to happen. Phillipa thought that relocating across the country would prove that point to Raya.

Besides, they both needed a fresh start. At least that's what Phillipa told herself. She refused to admit that she was running away again. She'd come home to be near her parents.

Being back home restored her a sense of security. It was something she hadn't felt in a long time. Yet, it also resurrected the unresolved anger she felt toward Kyle. Phillipa had been prepared to run into him from time-to-time in the precinct. She never expected she'd have to work with him daily. Having to work with him so closely spurred a whirlwind of emotions within her. She'd have to maintain her control.

The look she'd given him made Kyle Rossi's heart sink to his stomach. He sat at his desk, his thoughts consumed by Phillipa, whom he had affectionately nicknamed Philli when they were rookies. All these years, he'd been filled with regret over waiting a week before the wedding to admit he had cold feet.

Kyle had done what he thought was the honorable thing, tell the truth, despite how it had him in knots. He never expected her to just wish him well. She'd told him to get on with his life without her in it. Then Phillipa left town without giving Kyle a chance to explain that he never wanted to end the relationship; he only wanted to delay getting married until he felt more ready.

Despite so much time passing, Kyle had hoped to have a friendly reunion, but Phillipa's curt and frosty tone didn't seem to indicate that that was on the table.

"How do you like having your ex-fiancée as your boss?" his friend Bryant asked, dropping down in the empty chair beside his desk.

Shrugging in what he hoped was a nonchalant way, Kyle said, "I don't have a problem with it. I was the one who suggested to the captain that he reach out to Phillipa when Williams announced he was retiring."

Bryant looked surprised. "Really? I didn't know that. Does she know?"

Kyle shook his head. "I don't want her to ever find out. She didn't get the position because of me. She's good at her job." He'd suggested her because investigating cold cases was Phillipa's passion and her area of expertise.

"How do you know that?"

"She's been in the news a few times and is considered an expert in cold case investigations," he responded.

"You've been following her career?" Bryant asked.

"I've seen her listed as a facilitator at several different seminars over the years. Williams ran into her at a few times at conferences. He'd come back and remind me how I really messed up when I didn't marry Phillipa…like I didn't know that already."

"After the way things ended with you, you're not at all worried that she'll be out for some type of revenge?"

"Phillipa's not that kind of woman," he responded. "You ought to know that. You've known her almost as long as I have." They'd all joined the force at the same time.

"You haven't seen or talked to her in twelve years. People change, especially when they've been hurt. I will say that she's still a very beautiful woman."

"Yeah, she is," Kyle responded. Phillipa seemed even lovelier than before if that were at all possible. Her smooth complexion was the shade of sienna. Her dark curly hair, which was pulled into a low ponytail today, looked to be black, but he knew it was actually a dark shade of brown with subtle highlights throughout. Her eyes were an enticing mixture of brown and gold hues. Phillipa stood five inches shorter than his six-foot-two-inch height. The black fitted suit she wore looked classic and trendy at the same time.

"Maybe now the two of you will get back together."

Kyle thought of his earlier encounter with Phillipa and shook his head. "I don't think so…"

The phone on Bryant's desk rang, and he got up and walked across the floor to answer it.

Kyle turned his attention to a folder on his desk. The file contained the murder report of his sister-in-law, Helena, who was found murdered in 2010, leaving his brother and the rest of the family with questions as to who killed her and why.

Kyle hoped Phillipa could find those answers.

Phillipa stole a peek at the clock as she made her way back to her office from one of the conference rooms after a meeting with the reviewers.

She walked past the briefing room, which was also used for roll call and as a report writing area. Across the hall was a locker room and a workout area.

Down the hall at the other end was the evidence storage room.

In her office, Phillipa glanced down at her watch. It was almost three o'clock.

Her cell phone began to vibrate.

She picked it up and accepted the call. "Hey, sweetie. How was your first day at school?" She hoped Raya would come to love her new school. So far, she hated everything about Charlotte and didn't bother to hide it.

"It was good," her daughter responded. "I made a friend."

"I'm so glad to hear that." A wave of relief swept through her. Phillipa worried about Raya because she'd been adamant about staying in Los Angeles. Although she enjoyed spending time with her grandparents, the little girl hadn't wanted to leave her father or her friends behind.

"Mama, I'm happy we moved here."

"I'm really glad to hear that," Phillipa responded.

All Raya had done was cry when they first arrived two weeks ago. It thrilled her to see her daughter finally accepting that Charlotte was their home, and to watch her become acclimated.

"Grandma is gonna help me with my homework, so you don't have to do it after you come home."

"I love helping you."

"I'll tell Grandma that you're gonna help me with my math." Her voice became a low whisper. "She says she hasn't ever seen the kind of math we're being taught."

Phillipa chuckled. "Your grandmother's never been a fan of numbers, period. She loves history and English."

She talked for another minute, then said, "I need to get back to work, sweetie. Thanks for letting me know that you made it home. I'll see you in a couple of hours."

Phillipa placed her phone on her desk, then picked up a murder book to audit. It was a case that Kyle had recently closed. She'd already audited a few cases by some of the other detectives on her team and had purposely saved his case until last.

She stared out the window, reveling in the scenic view before her. The current climate in Charlotte was nice and warm. Phillipa would miss the year-round sunny weather of Los Angeles, especially when the temperature started to drop during the winter months. The thought of cold, bitter winds didn't thrill her, but having grown up in Charlotte, she was sure she'd re-adapt quickly.

With a sigh, Phillipa returned her attention to the murder book, opening it. She couldn't stall any longer.

Kyle was very thorough in his notes. She wasn't surprised. They'd attended the police academy together—it was where they'd met and fallen in love. Back then, he'd wanted to work in the Robbery Division. She wondered what changed his mind. Why had he chosen to become a homicide detective?

Phillipa waited until Kyle was gone before leaving for the day. She was relieved that he didn't linger around to attempt to strike up a conversation with her.

She quickly gathered up her things and walked out to her car.

Phillipa felt compelled to drive the short distance to Dillon Park, a five-acre park near uptown Charlotte. She drove through the entrance and past the greenway, a children's play area and a chapel. She didn't stop until she arrived at the gazebo. It was once her favorite place. She would come and sit there for hours, admiring the park's memorial rose garden.

It was the place where Kyle proposed to her. The chapel across the street was where they were supposed to exchange vows...

Phillipa wiped away a tear then got out of the vehicle.

She walked up to the beautiful white gazebo that was now stained with heartache and tragedy. Helena's body had been placed there after she was murdered.

Swallowing the chilling thought, Phillipa walked around the octagon-shaped pavilion, all the while wondering why the killer chose to leave Helena surrounded by roses in vivid hues of red, pink, yellow and white.

She sat down on the wooden bench, which used to be a place where she could clear her mind and gather a sense of peace and tranquility. Now all Phillipa felt was the palpable cloud of sadness that seemed to surround the gazebo.

She sat there for another twenty minutes before heading back to her car. She left the park and drove home. She didn't want Raya to worry. Some things were best left in the past, and right now she needed to focus on the present.

Chapter Two

When Kyle left the station, he drove straight to his brother's house. He turned into the cul-de-sac to find Jon outside playing ball with his thirteen-year-old twin daughters. He parked his car in the driveway.

As soon as he got out of the vehicle, the girls rushed Kyle, nearly knocking him to the ground.

Laughing, he embraced them. "You need to take it easy on your old uncle. I'm not as young as I used to be."

One of the girls frowned as she twirled one of her thin braids. "Why do people always say that? No one is as young as they used to be—we get older every year."

He glanced at Joi and chuckled. "How was your first day back at school?"

She gave a little shrug. "It was alright, Uncle K. I didn't get any homework. That's always great."

"Don't worry," Kyle couldn't resist adding. "You'll have some by the end of the week."

She made a face and groaned. "You just had to ruin it for me."

"I'm around to help, but I know how smart you are. You won't need me."

"Oh, I'll need your help with history."

He looked over at Toya and repeated the same question.

"It was fine. I *did* get homework. I have to write something unique about myself for my creative writing class."

"I'm sure you won't have a problem with that," Kyle responded with a smile. "You make jewelry and soaps. You've even sold some of them."

"Oh, yeah… I can write about that."

Jon sent the girls into the house, then asked, "Did you get a chance to talk to Philli about Helena's case?"

"Not yet, Jon," Kyle responded. "She wasn't exactly thrilled to see me. I stopped by her office to say hello and…well, I was met with a very cold reception. Philli can be a real ice queen."

Jon nodded. "I guess you can't blame her after what happened." His brother offered him a bottled water.

Unscrewing the top, Kyle responded, "I don't, but I'd like for us to get past it. We're working together and I don't want any tension between us."

"At some point, you two are going to have to sit down and talk," his brother said.

"I agree. Getting Philli to hear me out is going to be the challenge. She's always had a stubborn streak." Kyle placed the bottle to his lips to drink the cool, refreshing liquid.

"Well, I hope she'll agree to investigate Helena's murder. It's been twelve years and still no idea who murdered my wife. I won't be able to move past her death until I know her killer is behind bars."

His brother had never been able to accept that the police hadn't been able to find his wife's murderer and had closed her case. Kyle hoped Phillipa would agree to reopen it. He put the top back on the bottle. "I'll talk to Philli. I promise."

They navigated to the porch.

When Jon opened the front door, a female voice rang out. "I was just about to come get y'all. Dinner's already on the table."

Standing in the foyer, Amelie Rossi wiped her hands on her apron. She had moved in with her eldest son right after Helena was buried to help with the girls.

"Hey, Mom..." Kyle embraced her.

She brushed a graying tendril from her face. "Jon told me that you're going to be working with Phillipa. I didn't know she'd left California."

"They just moved back."

"*They?* She and her husband?"

"She and her daughter."

"What about her husband?"

"They're divorced," Kyle responded. He'd learned of Phillipa's divorce from her mother just a week before he'd put in her name as a replacement for his previous supervisor. Not that it changed anything—Phillipa was the right person for the job regardless. At least, that's what he told himself.

"I see... I'm not surprised though," Amelie said. "I could've told her that marriage wasn't gonna work. Phillipa's heart has always belonged to you. And yours to her."

"Mom, that was a long time ago."

"Do you still have feelings for her?" Jon asked.

Kyle gave a cautious non-answer before following his mother into the dining room. "I'll always care for her." But right now, his priority was working with her.

He needed to get her to trust him professionally, if not personally. He sat down across from Amelie. "Mom, the food smells delicious."

Amelie glanced back at him. "You sound like you're surprised."

He glimpsed the humor in her gaze and chuckled. "I know you're a phenomenal cook. Why do you think I always bring my appetite whenever I come by?"

"Pastor Brady asked me to make a couple of upside-down pineapple cakes for the bake sale on Saturday. He also wants me to make a lemon pound cake special for him."

"I've told Mom that Pastor Brady is sweet on her," Jon said.

"Hush that…" Amelie interjected. "That poor man lost his wife two years ago." Her eyes strayed to the girls, then back to Jon. "We don't need to have that kind of talk going on. Might give people the wrong idea."

Kyle bit back a smile when he caught the twins exchanging knowing glances. It was obvious to all of them that the pastor of Charlotte Christian Church was fond of Amelie.

"What about you, Uncle?" Joi asked. "When are you going to settle down and get married?"

"I have to meet the right woman first."

"He's met her, but your uncle let her slip away," Amelie stated. "I have a feeling that's about to change though. He might just get that second chance."

"Mom…"

"Well, she is back. If I were you, I'd try not to make the same mistake *twice*."

"Who is it?" Toya inquired. "Do we know her?"

"She met you girls a long time ago," Jon said.

"She's the lady Uncle K was gonna marry, right?" Joi asked. "I sure hope it's not Janice. I never liked her."

Amelie nodded. "I didn't care for Janice either. Her name is Phillipa Stevenson. She and your uncle were to be married, but when the wedding didn't happen, Phillipa left town, but now she's back. In fact, she works with Kyle."

"Oooh..." Joi uttered. "I can't wait to see how this is gonna turn out."

Kyle eyed her. "Really?" He couldn't believe his mother just put his past on blast like that.

"Yeah. It's *romantic*."

"Mom, don't let her read another one of your romance novels," he said.

Amelie smiled. "My books are sweet and wholesome. Besides, I happen to agree with Joi."

His mother had cooked a large pot of collards, turnips and mustard greens mixed together and served them with jalapeño corn bread. Nothing was as good as her greens and corn bread. There was also spiral sliced ham and potato salad, but Kyle could eat greens all day long.

"What did you do all day, Mom?" Kyle asked, hoping to get his family onto a topic other than him and Phillipa.

"I worked in the garden this morning," Amelie responded. "Then I went to the church to help put together care packages for the elderly. After that, I came home and started preparing dinner."

"Daddy, you were gone when we got up this morning. Did you have to do surgery?" Toya inquired.

"I did," Jon responded.

"Everything turn out good?" she asked.

"It did. My patient is doing well. In fact, I'm going back to the hospital after dinner to check on her."

Toya grinned. "I think I want to be a doctor when I grow up. I want to save lives like you, Daddy."

"Honey, you can be whatever you want," Jon responded.

"I'm still gonna study dance, too," Toya said.

Kyle bit back a smile. Just two days ago, his niece proclaimed she was going to be a dancer after attending a recital over the weekend. He loved that she was exploring her options.

He stayed until after they'd finished dessert, then went home and headed straight into a spare bedroom that served as his office. He sat down at his desk and turned on the computer.

He stared at the monitor, then picked up a folder containing copies of the investigative reports on his sister-in-law. Kyle hoped he could convince Phillipa to reopen the case despite the lack of witnesses or a suspect. A case without new information was not considered a priority for the unit. He hoped her fondness for Jon would be motivation enough for Phillipa to investigate.

After a frustrating hour, Kyle gave up. They didn't have any solid leads.

I'm missing something. He'd felt this way each time he looked through the file. Although his goal was to work in the Robbery Division, Kyle had come to CCU because he wanted to make sure Helena's murder didn't just occupy space on a shelf in a storage room.

He enjoyed his time in CCU. He'd closed several cases and it thrilled him to be able to go to a family and give them the answers they desperately needed. He sent up a silent prayer, asking God to provide closure for his family, too.

It was late when he finally shut his computer off, calling it a night.

Kyle took a shower, then prepared to watch some television before going to bed.

Instead, Phillipa entered his mind, spurring a wave of emotions in him. He was happy that she'd come home. And alone with his thoughts, he could admit that he was even happier that she was no longer attached to a husband. It wasn't that Kyle wanted to see her alone. But his heart had broken into several pieces—and so had his spirit—when he'd heard she was getting married.

At one time, he'd felt so strongly that he and Phillipa were supposed to be together for eternity. Even after she left town, Kyle never thought once that he wouldn't get her back. But she'd surprised him by falling in love with someone else. He shook his head, trying to evict Phillipa from his thoughts, and failing.

She was in his blood. They had so much history.

If only he could convince her to give him the opportunity to fully explain what happened twelve years ago. It might change her perception of him. Maybe, or maybe not, but Kyle had to try.

Phillipa locked away her duty weapon as soon as she arrived home, then prepared to join her family for dinner.

She was careful to avoid talking about her job while they ate. Instead, Phillipa enjoyed listening to Raya talk about her first day at her new school.

After dinner, she sent her daughter upstairs while she helped her mother in the kitchen.

An hour later, Phillipa sat on the edge of her daughter's bed while Raya sat at her desk applying clear nail polish to her fingernails. "Sweetie, did you really mean it when you said you're happy here?"

In the span of two months, Raya's father had announced that he was getting married and then Phillipa had hit her with the news that she'd taken a new position and they were relocating to North Carolina. She knew her daughter was probably overwhelmed by the abrupt changes in her life, but maybe one day Raya would see that this was all for the best.

Raya nodded. "Everybody is so nice. Even the ladies that work in the cafeteria. They let me have another juice when I asked, and I didn't have to pay for it. This boy in my class accidentally knocked over the first one."

"That was so sweet." Phillipa made a mental note to put a few more dollars on Raya's lunch account. "I'll make sure you have a little extra money for things like that."

"I can use it for my snacks."

"Not too many unless they're healthy snacks," she responded.

"That's all they have mostly," Raya said. "No candy but they do sell chocolate chip cookies."

Phillipa sat on the edge of the bed while talking to her daughter. "Did you complete all of your homework?"

"I did. Grandma checked it. It's in my backpack if you want to look at it too."

"I'm so very proud of you." Her heart swelled with love for her daughter.

"Why? What did I do?" Raya asked.

"I appreciate how mature you're behaving. I know it's been a lot of changes for you in a short time."

Raya glanced down at her hands. "I was afraid that I wouldn't make any friends, but everyone's been really nice."

Phillipa put a hand on her daughter's shoulder. "I have a feeling that you're going to make a lot of friends."

"Can I invite some girls over for my birthday? I kinda just want to do pizza and the movies. Nothing big."

"I believe I can manage that," Phillipa replied. Raya's birthday was three weeks away, so it gave her some time to plan something nice. She wanted her daughter to feel settled and at home here.

She stayed with Raya until she fell asleep.

"That granddaughter of mine is a real sweetheart," Bethany said when Phillipa went downstairs to the family room.

She sat down on the sofa beside her mother, who was removing the hairpins out of the bun at the nape of her neck. Bethany shared the same sienna-colored complexion as Phillipa. They also had the same brown eyes and nose. Phillipa thought the streak of gray at her mother's temple made her look even prettier, if that were possible.

"I was really worried about her when we left Los Angeles," Phillipa admitted. "But Raya seems to be adjusting well. And much sooner than I expected. She hasn't mentioned Gary or his wedding at all. I didn't know if I should bring it up."

"Does she get along with his fiancée?" Bethany worked through her long hair with a wide tooth comb.

"She did until Gary announced they were getting married. After that, Raya refused to be around the woman. That's another reason why I thought that moving here would be a good idea."

"How about you?" Bethany asked. "How do you feel about his getting remarried?"

"I'm happy for Gary," Phillipa responded. "He deserves someone who can be the type of wife he wants. I definitely wasn't it."

"Have you met the woman he plans to marry?"

"I did," Phillipa said. "Francine is nice enough."

"Have you seen Kyle yet?" Bethany questioned.

"I have. He's in my unit."

Her mother looked surprised. "Really?"

She nodded. "He was always interested in working in the Robbery Division. Mom, you can imagine my shock when I learned he was on my team."

Bethany nodded. "I hope you'll give him a fair chance, Phillipa."

She shrugged. "I'll treat Kyle the same way I treat the rest of the team."

"It's high time you sat down with him and talked."

"*About what?* He made himself clear back then."

"Phillipa, you were so angry with him—I'm not sure you really heard what Kyle was trying to tell you at the time."

"Mom, he waited until a week before the wedding to tell me that he didn't want to marry me. Trust me, I *heard* everything he had to say, and his words broke my heart." The humiliation and heartbreak she'd felt during that conversation was overwhelming. It had followed her for a long time after.

"How is your heart now?"

"Pieced together," Phillipa responded. "I don't think it will ever be whole again though." She knew now that she'd never be able to trust fully. It would never come as easily as it once had.

"How does Gary fit into all this?"

"I tried to make things work between us, but it just felt forced. Gary was a good husband. I wasn't as good a wife to him."

"Maybe once you forgive Kyle…"

She stiffened at Bethany's words. "I'm sorry, but that's never going to happen, Mom."

Phillipa was glad when her father walked into the house, putting an end to their conversation. She couldn't understand how her mother could be so forgiving toward him.

It stung like a betrayal.

"Hey, Dad…" she said as calmly as she could manage. "Just getting home from the office?" He was tall and muscular, in great shape for his years. Jacob often bragged that it was because of the time he spent playing golf.

He nodded. "My meeting with my clients ran longer than I'd planned. It's a good thing though—there was some surprising evidence that came up."

Jacob bent down to plant a kiss on his wife's forehead.

"Are you hungry?" Bethany inquired. "I can make you a sandwich."

He shook his head. "We ate during the meeting. I had my secretary pick up some food for us."

Phillipa stood. "I'm going up to bed. I'll see y'all in the morning."

"I wanted to hear how your first day went."

"Dad, I'll tell you over breakfast." She smiled softly and left the room.

Upstairs, she opened the door to her closet and walked inside, figuring she'd pick out her work clothes for tomorrow. Phillipa couldn't decide between the gray pin-striped suit or the one in green. She finally decided on a pair of black slacks. *I'll figure out the rest of the outfit when I wake up.*

She showered, then slipped on a pair of pajama pants and a tank top. Phillipa fashioned her hair into a loose braid, then climbed into bed. She was tired, but not sleepy. If only the nervous energy churning around in her stomach would stop.

Phillipa wished she could bury herself in work, but she knew it wouldn't be enough to ward off the thoughts of Kyle that infiltrated her mind too often to keep track of. Over the years, she'd tried to forget him—wipe him from her memory banks—but to no avail.

After they broke up, Phillipa, without hesitation, was fast out the door, leaving Kyle holding the engagement ring he'd given her. Instead of pleading with her to stay, he simply took a step back and wished her well.

She wasn't sure which hurt most. Calling off the wedding or his not caring whether he'd ever see her again.

The next morning, Kyle waited until after the unit meeting ended to approach Phillipa. He wasn't in any hurry to surround himself with her chilly presence, but he'd promised Jon.

He knocked on the open door, saying, "May I speak with you, Sergeant Stevenson?"

She eyed him warily before answering. "Sure. C'mon in."

He could feel the temperature drop the moment he stepped into the room, evidenced by the rapid spread of chill bumps on his arms.

Phillipa looked stunning in a pale purple shirt beneath a tan-and-purple-striped blazer paired with black slacks. Except for a few escaping spirals, her curly hair was tamed into a low bun. Her badge hung around her neck on a chain.

"What did you want to discuss?"

"Do you remember Helena?" he asked after taking a seat in an empty chair facing her desk.

Her eyes turned sad. "I do," Phillipa replied. "I was really sorry to hear of her death. My heart goes out to Jon and their children."

"The twelve-year anniversary is coming up soon. I wanted to ask if you'd review the case… Actually, my brother would like you to look at it personally." Kyle placed a thick folder on her desk.

"How is Jon?"

"He misses Helena," Kyle responded. "The girls miss their mother. Philli—"

"Please don't call me that," she interjected.

"My apologies," he uttered. "Jon needs some kind of closure, and he won't have that until his wife's killer is brought to justice."

"What can you tell me about this case?" Phillipa asked.

Kyle pulled his chair closer to the desk. "Helena was last seen around August eighth—about twenty days before she was found in the gazebo at Dillon Park. Someone shot her."

Kyle's eyes never left her face. He could almost read her thoughts. The gazebo in Dillon Park used to be a favorite place of hers. How ironic that his sister-in-law's body was found in the very place he'd proposed to Phillipa.

"That was about three months after I left town."

He nodded in agreement. Three months after his decision to call off the wedding.

"Are there any witnesses?" she asked. "A known suspect?"

"No," Kyle responded. "It's a priority four." Usually only the cases ranked priority one and two were reinvestigated. The chance of even a priority three case being reopened depended on the availability of certain lab results.

She eyed him. "Priority four cases aren't normally reopened unless there's been new information."

"I know."

"Has there been any new information?"

"No."

Phillipa opened the folder and quickly scanned the contents. "I'll need to see everything. Is the file organized?"

"Does this mean that you'll reopen the case?"

"I'd like to be able to give your brother some answers and get justice for Helena. But I'll need to evaluate the file and see if I can generate any viable leads. I'll let you know what I decide."

Kyle smiled. "Thank you. Jon and I both appreciate this. If you decide to reopen the case, I'll be glad to help with the investigation."

"No… I don't need your help." Phillipa laid the folder down on her desk, then asked, "As a matter of fact, how long have you been with this unit?"

"A couple of years now," Kyle responded.

"Detectives assigned to cold cases should not only have a background in death investigation, but also be

well versed in how to obtain old records and have knowledge of current scientific testing methods."

He tensed. "Are you questioning my qualifications?"
he asked. "Because I have both the education and the
experience, Sergeant Stevenson. I'm sure you have a
copy of my personnel file."

She didn't respond.

He huffed. "I want you to know that I hate this tension between us. We need to talk about what happened.
You can get whatever you're feeling off your chest."

"That's not necessary," Phillipa stated. "I'll get back
to you with my decision once I review Helena's case."

Kyle stood up. "Thanks again."

"Oh, I need Jon's number. I would like to speak with
him."

He bent down and quickly wrote it on a Post-it note.
"Here you go."

Kyle released a satisfied sigh as he left Phillipa's office. He sent up a quick prayer asking God once again to
intercede on Helena's behalf. His family wanted to find
the person responsible for killing her. He also prayed
that Phillipa wouldn't let her anger and bitterness toward him keep her from reopening the case. He'd never
known her to be vindictive, but she could've changed
over the years. Kyle had hoped her anger would have
abated some after twelve years, but clearly it hadn't.

It wasn't that he felt he was owed her forgiveness.
While he'd never set out to hurt Phillipa, he tried to
avoid what he thought might turn out to be a mistake
in getting married too soon.

He simply didn't think he was ready for what was
supposed to be a lifelong commitment despite his love
for Phillipa. Kyle had felt a flurry of confusion in the

weeks leading up to the wedding. It began when his mentor, an assistant pastor at the church, had confessed to having an affair. He'd advised Kyle to wait and be sure he was ready for marriage.

He'd followed that advice…and lost Phillipa forever.

Chapter Three

She watched Kyle walk out of her office, then released the breath she was holding. Phillipa knew that forgiveness was required by God, and she'd honestly tried to get past her heartbreak, but it was still a huge struggle for her.

She'd found a way to accept what happened, but Phillipa wasn't free of the anger that had taken up permanent residence in her heart. She'd prayed to God for years, asking Him to put an end to her pain. But her pleas were met with silence. She felt she'd been abandoned by both the man who'd promised to love her forever and the heavenly Father who'd vowed He'd never leave her.

She had a right to her bitterness.

Phillipa picked up a photo of Helena and thought of the gazebo. It was such a beautiful place that was now marred by tragedy.

She recalled attending the wedding festivities of Jon and Helena and their subsequent baby shower as Kyle's girlfriend. She and Helena never ran in the same circles and were only around one another during the Rossi family gatherings, but the woman was always kind to her. Helena worked as an accountant for a special events company and had graciously connected Phillipa with one of the bridal consultants to help plan the wedding that never took place.

She felt terrible for Jon. It had to be pure torment to live all these years in a cruel limbo of mourning, hoping for answers that had never come. Phillipa vowed to do what she could to help him find closure, even if it meant teaming up with Kyle.

When Phillipa evaluated a cold case file, she looked specifically for any evidence that could benefit from modern investigative methods and forensic testing. In this instance, she would check to see if there was any fingerprint evidence collected. If there was, the first thing Phillipa planned to do was resubmit it for testing with the hope that current technology could expand upon the prior test results.

Sadly, there wasn't any.

She'd worked a few cases where the evidence collected had disappeared or was damaged somehow in the evidence room. In some cases, detectives believed a case was fully investigated and discarded some of the evidence because space was needed to store files from other cases.

She reviewed all the evidence that had been recovered, which wasn't much. All the investigators concluded that Helena had been killed in one location and her body moved to the gazebo.

Phillipa couldn't help but wonder if there was some significant meaning behind it. She wrote the word *gazebo* on a notepad with a question mark.

Helena had been shot in the chest, and two bullets

removed from her. Phillipa checked to see if they had been run through the National Integrated Ballistic Information Network.

She discovered that they hadn't been—not back then. When the murder took place, the police department didn't use NIBIN because of budgetary restraints. Phillipa decided to run it through the database to compare the casings against all the other guns already logged. Even if there wasn't a match, the information would be stored away for future use.

I really want to do this for Jon. He's always been a good friend. But I've got to do this by the book and find something to justify reopening Helena's case.

Phillipa glanced outside.

She could see a squad car and a detective's cruiser turning onto the street. The plaza and parking lot down below was flooded with officers, some in uniform and others in street clothes, coming and going.

The sounds of phones ringing and people talking echoed in the hallway. Phillipa heard snippets of voices raised in protest coming from visitors as they were escorted to interrogation rooms.

Phillipa turned her attention back to the file on her desk.

It would be so much easier if there was some type of rock-solid lead on the perp, but they didn't have one.

I'm just going to have to look deeper into Helena's life. Hopefully I'll find something.

It was not going to be easy getting through to Phillipa, Kyle decided. He knew her well enough to know that she wasn't going to budge an inch if she didn't have a mind to—she'd always been stubborn.

But Kyle had every confidence she would investigate Helena's case in a professional capacity. He knew Phillipa wouldn't take out her disappointment in him on Jon.

Why did she have to be so beautiful? Age had had no effect on Phillipa—she had taken extremely good care of herself, it was obvious. And her daughter was the spitting image of her. He had seen her photograph on the desk. She would grow up to be another beauty.

Kyle was curious as to why Phillipa's marriage had ended in divorce, though it was not something he could ever ask her—not if he wanted to keep his head attached to his body. The thought brought a smile to his lips. Phillipa had always had a fiery temper. As strange as it might seem to others, it was one of the things he loved most about her. She was a fighter—no, a survivor. It was those qualities that had gotten Phillipa through the police academy. He admired her tough-as-nails attitude.

She had no idea how much he regretted his actions. How he was all set to go after her until he found out she was about to marry another man. Knowing she was about to share her life and give her love to someone else had felt like torture to Kyle. Phillipa may not think so, but he knew what it meant to have a broken heart.

When he'd heard from Bethany that Phillipa was divorced, Kyle couldn't deny that he was secretly thrilled by the news, but then guilt had quickly washed over him. He had no right to celebrate what had to have been a painful decision for her and her husband to make.

Now that she was back in Charlotte, Kyle took it as a sign that God had finally answered his prayers. Phillipa was the only woman he'd ever loved, and if given the chance to be in her life once more, in any capacity, he vowed not to take it for granted.

* * *

Phillipa's heart sank when she read that Helena was pregnant when she'd died. Her eyes filled with tears, and she wiped them with the back of her hands.

Two lives lost... Such a tragedy.

She was still trying to accept that the sweet woman she used to see with Jon was dead.

Phillipa couldn't imagine Helena having an enemy in the world. She searched and scanned cases to see if there had been any other victims found around that same time frame, looking for some sort of connection.

Nothing.

Questions formed in her mind: Was Helena targeted? Stalked? Who would want her dead?

Phillipa returned to her original theory that the killing was personal. She would have to ask Jon about any enemies Helena might have had. The woman she remembered didn't do much outside of work and church. She seemed to enjoy being at home. It was clear that she loved her role as a wife and mother. The twins had been toddlers when Phillipa had left town. They'd lost their mother so young.

The first thing she needed to do was speak with Jon. Phillipa wanted some insight on Helena from the person who knew her best—her husband. She hoped the conversation would spark something that might turn into a clue as to what was going on in Helena's life before she was killed.

She looked up and caught Kyle watching her. She had a clear view of his work area. Phillipa quickly averted her gaze.

I wish I'd known he worked in CCU. I never would've taken this job.

She silently chided herself for being so juvenile in her thinking. This position was a good one with opportunity for advancement. Plus, she was closer to her parents—something Phillipa had wanted for a long time. She had grown tired of life in Los Angeles.

I can do this.

Phillipa prided herself on her ability to keep her personal and professional lives separate. She was Kyle's supervisor. She could handle him. She would treat him as any other employee.

I can DO this.

She stole a peek at Kyle.

He was seated at his desk talking to someone on the telephone. Phillipa watched him longer than she'd planned to before forcing her gaze away and back to the stack of files cluttering her desk. She intended to clear all of them by the time she left for the day.

Chapter Four

Before she left the precinct at the end of her shift, Phillipa placed a quick call to Jon.

"Hey, this is Phillipa. I'd like to drop by to discuss Helena's case. Is now a good time for you?"

"That'll be great. I'm leaving the hospital now and will be home all evening," he responded. "My mom and the girls will be heading to Bible Study in about fifteen minutes."

"I'll see you in thirty."

Kyle was still at his desk when Phillipa left her office. As much as she wanted to ignore his presence, she couldn't be that rude. It would be unprofessional on her part.

Although she didn't have to tell him, Phillipa approached his desk and said, "I'm on my way to see your brother."

He smiled. "That's good. He's looking forward to seeing you."

She couldn't think of anything else to say, other than "Enjoy your evening, Kyle."

"You, too."

Phillipa resisted the urge to glance over her shoulder, to take one last look at his handsome face.

Minutes later, she keyed Jon's address in the GPS, then drove out of the parking lot.

Right before she'd left town, Jon had completed a cardiothoracic surgery fellowship. Twelve years later, he was now a prominent heart surgeon.

She soon realized that he didn't live too far from her parents' neighborhood, where she now lived, too. Phillipa glanced around, admiring the manicured lawns and stately homes.

Jon was still dressed in hospital scrubs when she arrived. He had an athletic build like Kyle. They possessed the same warm brown eyes and full lips, and their biggest difference was that Jon's complexion was a couple shades lighter than his brother's.

"Did you just get home?" Phillipa asked.

"I walked in about ten or fifteen minutes ago." He gave her a friendly hug. "Wow, you haven't aged a day since the last time I laid eyes on you."

Phillipa chuckled. "Sweet but totally untrue."

"I mean it… You look great."

"Thank you, Jon. So do you."

"Despite everything," he uttered. "When Helena died, I felt like I'd aged fifty years."

She smiled in commiseration, though she couldn't imagine what he'd been through. They sat down in the living room.

"I was beyond happy when Kyle told me you were going to be taking over the Cold Case Unit," Jon said. "I've been very frustrated with the investigators in the past. I felt like they didn't care. Nobody really looked into the case much until Kyle transferred into the unit."

"I spoke with Matt Conway, the assistant district attorney, about reopening the case. I want to assure you that we'll do everything possible to find the person or persons responsible," Phillipa said. "That's why I'm here. I'd like to ask you some questions."

"Okay."

"I realize it's been twelve years, but what can you tell me about Helena's state of mind in the days leading up to her death?"

"She seemed to be worried about something, but every time I tried to get her to talk to me, she wouldn't. When I found out about the baby, I figured that's what was bothering her. Helena and I had always planned on having two children—we got twins the first time around, so we agreed that we were done. When she got pregnant that second time...she didn't tell me."

"So you found out—"

"When they performed the autopsy," Jon interjected.

"Did you notice her acting strangely?"

"Like I mentioned earlier, she seemed worried about something, but that's all."

"I read in the file that Helena disappeared from the parking lot at work. There weren't any security cameras?"

"Not in the back. From what her friend Paula told me, Helena was taking the trash out—only, she never returned. No one saw anything." He paused. "That day, it was heavy on my heart to stop by her job. I was going to, but I had an emergency at the hospital. I couldn't leave. Maybe if I'd left..."

Helena gently placed a hand on his arm. "Don't torture yourself, Jon. It wasn't your fault."

He sighed. "I should've let another doctor do the surgery."

"You didn't do anything wrong. There wasn't any way for you to know something would happen."

"I want that murderer found," Jon uttered. He leaned back in his chair. "Sometimes I worry he'll come back for my girls. I haven't rested well since that horrible day."

She wanted to help Jon and his daughters find peace. "I'm going to give this case my full attention."

He smiled. "I know you will. I'm glad you're back."

"It's so good to see you." Phillipa stood up. "I'd better head home to check on Raya."

He walked her to the door. "You have to see the girls sometime. They're thirteen now. I have to confess that I feel ill-equipped to handle two teenagers."

"I understand. My daughter will soon be eleven going on sixteen," Phillipa responded with a chuckle. "I'm not ready…"

"If my mother wasn't here, I don't know what I'd do. I always ask myself, what would Helena do in this situation? Teenage girls are so emotional—at least that's been my experience."

"I'm sure you're doing a great job. And you have a wonderful support system with your mother and Kyle."

It was clear that Jon was still very much in love with Helena, despite her being gone twelve years. That was the kind of love Phillipa thought she'd had with his brother. A type of love that not even death could destroy—an endless love.

But Kyle didn't love her enough to go through with their marriage. He couldn't handle a lifetime commitment. Even now, he remained a bachelor.

Still unable to commit.

Just the thought of Kyle summoned up the painful memories of their past, and working with him made it even harder to forget the hurt he had caused her.

When would the heartache end?

Kyle had resisted the urge to walk into the house and interrupt Jon's meeting with Phillipa when he passed by thirty minutes ago. Instead, he drove the two blocks to his own place. He knew Jon would call him before the night was over to update him.

One of the reasons Kyle had chosen to work in the Cold Case Unit over Robbery was because of his brother. He wanted to make sure Helena's case didn't remain unsolved. He didn't want Jon to spend the rest of his life wondering what happened to his wife. Kyle didn't want that for any of the victims—only, this one was more personal. He enjoyed his work, and each time he closed a case, he felt fulfilled.

He parked his work vehicle in the driveway and got out. His SUV, a Cadillac, and a Mercedes-AMG SLC 43, his baby, took up space in the two-car garage.

As Kyle walked up the steps to the porch, he felt the familiar strings of loneliness tugging at him. He yearned for companionship—he missed Phillipa because she was the only woman who really got him. Kyle often wondered how he had ever let her get away. Yet his reasons had been sound. He hadn't felt ready for marriage and had loved her enough to be honest about those feelings. It didn't take Kyle long to recognize that what he wanted most was a life with Phillipa. However, by then it was too late.

Despite that, Kyle wasn't about to beg her to let him

back in her life. They would work together and be civil, and that was all he would ask for.

It still stung him deeply that she'd left town and then so easily married another man six months after they'd broken up. Clearly, Phillipa hadn't been as heartbroken as she wanted him to believe. Kyle was glad to have her back in Charlotte, but he didn't have a clue as to how to pick up the pieces of what they once had. He had to accept that he'd lost her forever. He hoped that they could eventually rebuild their friendship at least.

Phillipa pulled into an empty space inside the three-car garage where her parents kept their cars. Before closing the door, she paused a moment to admire her mother's amazing rose bushes. Bethany Jones loved roses, and breeding hybrid roses was a hobby of hers.

The custom-built brick home sat on a two-acre corner lot in Mint Hill. Phillipa entered the house through the mudroom entrance. She walked toward the two-story foyer, and placed her tote on a table near the stairs. Her parents' bedroom was on the main level, while she and Raya occupied two of the four bedrooms on the second floor. Phillipa headed to the gourmet kitchen which featured an oversize island, sprawling granite countertops and a large pantry. A bright sunroom opened directly into the backyard.

"Hey, Mama," Raya greeted her from a stool at the kitchen's island. "You came home just in time. I made dinner."

"*You* made dinner," Phillipa said. "Wow…this is a treat."

"You might not think so when I tell you what I cooked."

"What's on the menu?"

"Sloppy joes," Raya responded with a chuckle.

"Yum…" Phillipa murmured. "You're taking me back to my college days."

"I remember you telling me that. When I saw a packet for it at the grocery store earlier, I told Grandma I wanted to cook that for you. She showed me how to make it from scratch."

"I'm so glad you did. It's still one of my favorites."

Raya smiled. "It smells so good. I can't wait to try it."

Phillipa frowned. "I never made them for you?"

"No, you didn't."

"Sloppy joes are addictive."

"I can handle it, Mama."

She hugged her daughter. "Thanks so much for being so thoughtful, sweetie. Where are your grandparents?"

"Grandma went to check on the laundry and Granddad is in his office. I think he's on the phone with a client. Lawyers work as much as police officers."

"Yes, they do."

"Dad's a lawyer, but he didn't work like that," Raya went on.

"That's because he's a corporate attorney. Your grandfather is a litigation lawyer. He helps people win lawsuits."

"I don't want to be a lawyer or a police detective. Y'all work too much."

Phillipa chuckled. "Little lady, you can be whatever you want. You're very lucky to have so many options."

"I love art."

"I know you do."

"What would you say if I told you that I want to be an artist?"

"I'd say go for it," Phillipa responded. "I read that one of the colleges here offers an art camp each year. If you like, we can register you next summer."

"I'd love it."

A few minutes later, her parents joined them at the dinner table. After her father blessed the food, Phillipa bit into her meat-stuffed bun. "This is soooo good," she said after a moment. "It's the right combination of sweet and tangy. You did a great job, Raya."

"It *is* good," Raya murmured. "I can see why you like it so much. I can't believe you never made this for me. This is now my favorite food. After macaroni and cheese."

"You are definitely your mother's child," Bethany said. "She used to love macaroni and cheese, too."

Phillipa chuckled. "I still do."

"I have to say I haven't had a sloppy joe sandwich since I don't know when," Jacob stated.

Bethany wiped her mouth on the edge of a napkin. "It was probably when Phillipa was in high school. It's been a long time. I'm surprised I remembered all the ingredients."

"Woman, you have the memory of an elephant," her husband responded.

After dinner, Phillipa helped Raya with her homework.

"I don't like science," her daughter declared.

"I didn't either until I was in high school," she told Raya.

"Mom…are you glad you came back to Charlotte?" That was a shift in topic, but Phillipa made a point to always be honest with her daughter.

"I am. I needed this," Phillipa said.

"Is it because Daddy is marrying Francine?" Raya asked.

"No, it had nothing to do with that." Phillipa shifted to face her daughter. "Honey, how do you feel about your dad getting married?"

"I always thought he'd come back home."

"That was never going to happen, Raya," Phillipa said as gently as she could. "Your dad and I really feel that it's best for all of us if we lead separate lives."

"It's not best for me."

"Would you want to live with two unhappy people?"

"No."

"That's what it would be like."

Raya looked up at her. "You really don't love Dad anymore?"

"I'll always care about him, but no… I'm not in love with him."

Her daughter didn't respond.

"You're too young to understand, sweetie. Please remember that we both love you. Your dad loves Francine, and he wants to build a home with her. There will be one more person in our lives who loves you."

"I guess…"

"I thought you liked Francine."

"I do. I just thought Daddy would miss us and come home."

Phillipa hugged her daughter. "Everything will be fine. You'll see."

Long after everyone had gone to bed, Phillipa sat at her father's desk, thoroughly going through Helena's murder book. She began with the chronological record of the investigation, which provided a brief description of what was investigated, the detective's actions and what may need further investigation later. She noted the name of the detective who authored the entry. Phillipa found that he was organized enough in his notes for her to understand how the initial investigation had progressed.

She reviewed the crime scene log next. Phillipa read the twenty-four-hour homicide report made by the primary investigator, which contained victim information, witness information, a summary of their statements and a synopsis of the crime, including modus operandi. Helena's file also contained crime scene photographs.

She'd already reviewed the death, autopsy and forensic reports before talking to Jon.

There were a few issues that could be problematic. First, the primary detective who'd worked the case was now deceased. That meant any evidence he might have collected would be a challenge to get admitted into court. But Phillipa was going to do her best. Helena's husband and daughters were counting on her.

Over the years, she'd met with so many family members, and like with Jon, she witnessed their hurt and the torment brought on by the lack of answers. Phillipa really wanted to bring some sort of resolution to Jon. And the sooner, the better.

"I'm going to find out who did this and why," she whispered. "You didn't deserve to die this way."

She glanced at the clock and was surprised to see it was after midnight. Still, Phillipa spent another hour writing out her own notes on the case before going up to her bedroom.

She changed into a pair of shorts and a tank top before brushing her teeth and washing her face. Then

Phillipa pulled her hair up into a bun, slipped on a silk bonnet and climbed into bed.

She lay there staring up at the ceiling for a few minutes before sitting up.

Phillipa eased out of bed and sat on the bench in her room. She focused in on a painting of a lake over the fireplace and tried to quiet her racing thoughts. She replaced disturbing ones with pleasant images of frolicking on the beach with Raya, sitting in the park watching her daughter play soccer and watching Disney movies—happy memories. Phillipa didn't like to go to bed with a sense of heaviness weighing on her. Mindfulness techniques often helped.

Right before she got back in bed, Phillipa's gaze landed on the Bible her mother had placed on the nightstand. She felt the tug to open it but ignored the pull, turning away instead. She and God were not exactly on speaking terms at the moment. He required forgiveness, and where Kyle was concerned, this was something she just couldn't give him. Not even for God.

Phillipa turned to her left side and closed her eyes, hoping sleep would soon come. She was tired physically and mentally, but she didn't feel drowsy. In fact, she felt wide awake.

An hour passed, then another.

Phillipa tried listening to an app on her phone. Sometimes the sound of a thunderstorm did the trick, but not tonight.

She switched to soft jazz, hoping the music would lull her to sleep.

Another hour came and went.

Phillipa groaned in frustration as she turned to her right side. It was going to be one of those nights. The kind where Kyle invaded her mind without invitation. In the past, it was easy enough to dismiss thoughts of him, but now that she saw him daily, it had become a challenge.

She found herself wondering if Kyle had any of the same struggles she experienced whenever it came to working together. He'd mentioned clearing the air but there wasn't anything Kyle could say that could undo the heartbreak she felt.

Chapter Five

Kyle caught up with Phillipa when she arrived the next day. He was on his way to the break room for coffee when he saw her. She wore an emerald green suit with a cream shirt underneath and a pair of medium-heeled nude pumps. He knew she kept a pair of flats in her tote because they were always peeking out. She had on a pair of black-framed glasses. He remembered that Phillipa usually wore them whenever she stayed up late the night before. As always, her hair was pulled away from her face, this time in a ponytail. He longed to see her long locks flowing free.

Kyle immediately shook away the thought and said, "Phillipa, I want to say thanks again for your help."

"It's not necessary," she responded. "I'm happy to do what I can to get Jon some answers."

"I'm grateful and still willing to help."

"Absolutely not," Phillipa uttered in response. "Kyle, I don't need your help. Besides, you already have a heavy caseload."

"I can't just sit by and do nothing," he responded. "I

may not be your favorite person, but I love my brother and I hate seeing him in pain like this."

Kyle caught a glimmer of sadness in her eyes. He prayed that she'd find a way to forgive him because he still cared deeply for her.

"I understand, Kyle," she said, her tone softening a bit. "I really do, but you said yourself that Jon wanted *me* to investigate Helena's murder. If I have questions for you or need your help, I'll come to you. I know how much this means to you both."

He gave a slight nod.

"I'll definitely let you know everything I learn."

"I appreciate that," Kyle responded.

"Actually…maybe you can answer a couple of questions for me. What do you remember about Helena during the time leading up to her disappearance?"

"I didn't see her or Jon much. I was working a lot," he said. "Jon thought something was bothering her—he did tell me that."

"He mentioned it to me as well. Jon said he just assumed it was about the pregnancy."

"They only planned to have two children, but I don't know why Helena would've been worried about that. My brother wouldn't have treated a third child any different," Kyle responded.

"There's a chance that what was bothering Helena had nothing to do with the baby," Phillipa said.

"I agree," he responded. "We just don't have any leads."

"I'm going to find something. We need to post her photo on social media and ask for the community's help. I know it's on the CMPD website with the Crime Stoppers tip line, but we need to make sure it's everywhere.

The unit has solved forty-nine cases since it was created in 2003. I'd like to clear that number before this year ends."

"That's ambitious," Kyle said. "But I'll certainly do what I can to make it happen."

"It's not so much about achieving numbers for bragging rights—I'm thinking of the families who will finally have closure if we can get these cases solved."

He nodded in agreement.

"I guess I need to get started. Helena has waited long enough for justice."

Kyle watched Phillipa make her way to her workspace.

She was special indeed.

Half an hour later, Phillipa frowned as she stared at the computer screen in her office. There didn't seem to be much information about Helena before she'd married Jon. She searched her memory, trying to recall where Helena had lived before moving to Charlotte.

Phillipa couldn't remember, so she got up and walked to the door, hating to ask Kyle anything. She didn't want his aid in solving this case, didn't want to work that closely with him, but she couldn't deny he might prove to be useful. He was intelligent, and according to his performance evaluations and the cases he touched, Kyle possessed great investigative instincts.

She gestured for him to join her in her office.

"Do you happen to know where Helena was born?" Phillipa asked when Kyle entered and took a seat in one of the empty visitor chairs across from her desk.

"Atlanta," he responded. "Why?"

"I haven't been able to find much about her. Her life before she came to Charlotte seems pretty vague."

"The last investigator didn't find much either," Kyle responded. "But I don't think he was able to fully focus on the case because he had cancer and ended up going on medical leave."

"I did pull up a Georgia birth certificate for Helena Douglas—but the year doesn't match. It could be a typo, but I would think it would've been corrected at some point."

Kyle looked as puzzled as she was. "What about her birth date? Did it match?"

"Yes. Only the year was off. Unless she was lying about her age. According to this, she'd be two years older than we believed."

"That would put her the same age as Jon," he stated. "I don't see a reason why she'd lie about that. Must have been a typo. She would have had to have it amended to get her passport and other legal documents. I can give Jon a call to see if he has a copy in the safe. Unless you'd rather make the call."

"It's fine if you do it. See if he can send it over ASAP."

"If he's not at home, I'm sure my mom can get it for us."

"That would be great. Thanks, Kyle." Phillipa chewed on her bottom lip before adding, "What I remember about Helena is that she was pretty much a homebody. Did that ever change?"

He shook his head. "Helena basically only went to work and church, unless she was going somewhere with Jon."

"What about friends?"

"She was close to a girl she worked with. Paula Johnson."

Phillipa watched Kyle's expression change when he mentioned Helena's friend. She wondered if he'd dated Paula. She felt an unexpected stab of jealousy prick at her.

"Since Helena died, Paula's been trying to cozy up to Jon."

She continued to study him. "I take it you don't care for her."

"I don't," Kyle responded. "I never believed she was a real friend to Helena. I could tell from the moment I met her that Paula only had eyes for Jon."

"Do you think she'd try to harm Helena?"

He shook his head. "No. She's all of five-two and very thin. There's no way she could've moved Helena's body to the gazebo."

"She could've had help," Phillipa offered. "If what you said is true, it could be a motive."

"Paula hates guns with a passion. She almost freaks out at the mention of one. Jon said that she lost a brother to gun violence when they were in their teens."

"I'd still love to have a conversation with her."

"She's a nuisance, sure enough, but a killer…no, I don't think so." Kyle stood up. "I'll call Jon about the birth certificate."

"Thanks," Phillipa said. "Oh, did you ever meet any of Helena's family? I remember at the wedding, there were only a few people seated on the bride's side at the church."

"She always said she was an only child and that her family was very small. Come to think of it, there was a cousin of hers that came to the wedding. Helena introduced us."

Picking up her pen, Phillipa asked, "Do you remember the name?"

"I don't. It was a long time ago. Jon and I went through her contact list when she died—there weren't many names in it—just local people."

It struck Phillipa as odd that Helena didn't have any family members listed in her address book. "Was she on social media?"

"No," Kyle said. "Helena was extremely private. She wouldn't even sign a photo release at church. She would get upset if someone took her picture without permission."

A few minutes later, after she'd asked him a couple more questions about Helena but didn't really learn anything new, Kyle left the office.

Phillipa picked up a photo of Helena from the file. "If I'm going to find your killer, I need your help."

She pulled up the birth certificate once more, then opened another window on the computer. Phillipa conducted a search on Helena's parents.

"They had four children," she murmured to herself upon finding the results. "Helena had three siblings. She wasn't an only child."

These inconsistencies weren't enough to justify reopening the case, but it was enough to ignite her interest in learning more about Helena.

"Here is a copy of the birth certificate Helena had," Kyle said a few hours later, stepping into her office doorway. "Looks like it was amended."

"Then there should be a certified copy on file, but

there isn't." Phillipa compared the two. "The date was changed on the one that was in Helena's possession."

She studied it for a moment, then stated, "It's a counterfeit."

Phillipa handed it to Kyle. "Take a good look at them both and tell me what you see."

"It's really hard to detect fake birth certificates most times," he said. "But looking at these…everything but the year is the same."

"Take a closer look."

Kyle glanced up at Phillipa and said, "The year is a different font. If she'd realized the error and asked to have it corrected, Helena would've been issued a new one. The agency wouldn't have just changed the year. It would be a completely new birth certificate."

"There's something else. I did a search on her parents, and they had three other children."

Kyle's brow creased as he appeared to take in that information. "Maybe she didn't get along with them," he offered. "Maybe there was a rift, so Helena never talked about them."

Phillipa picked up the birth certificate once again and stared at it. Something just didn't feel right.

"I need to verify whether there's an amended copy somewhere in the system," she said.

"If it exists, I'm sure you'll find it," Kyle responded.

Phillipa wasn't so sure. She hadn't expected these new discoveries about Helena. But she appreciated Kyle's faith in her, nonetheless.

Chapter Six

Bryant walked out of Phillipa's office that afternoon and addressed Kyle. "She wants to see you."

"For what?" Kyle asked.

"She's been auditing our cases."

He sighed softly in resignation.

She's going to point out every mistake I've made. So this is her way of pushing me out of the department.

Kyle reproached himself for letting the thought form. Phillipa was more of a professional than this.

"You wanted to see me?" he asked her a minute later, standing in her office doorway.

"I did."

He sat down facing her.

Phillipa cleared her throat softly before saying, "Detective Rossi, I've reviewed several of the cases you worked on, and I have to say that you've done an outstanding job," she said. "I need to give you props. It seems you've put in tireless work to resolve open cases and bring some degree of resolution to the victims and their families. Thank you for all you've done and continue to do in this department."

Relief bloomed in him, and warmth at her words. "I can't take all the credit. We work as a team in this unit. It's not just one person."

She awarded him a smile. "I initially had doubts about you being here, but I was wrong."

"I appreciate you saying that," Kyle responded. If he was being honest with himself, Phillipa had had him a bit concerned that she'd try to get him out of the department with her initial comments about his credentials.

She broke into a short laugh. "I can see from your expression that you thought I'd be vindictive and try to sabotage you in some way."

"I did think so initially, but deep down I knew you weren't that type of person."

"How can you be so sure?" she asked. "To be honest, I really did consider looking for every mistake you've made and forcing you to leave."

"But you didn't do it—it's not you." Kyle paused a heartbeat, then said, "Would you please have dinner with me tonight? We should talk about the past so we can finally lay it to rest."

Her demeanor changed from one of warmth to a sudden coolness. "I have plans with my parents and my daughter."

"Are you okay with the way we are?" he asked. "Because I'm not."

"I didn't do this," Phillipa responded tersely. "The reality is that there's nothing you can say to me that will change what happened. Or make me feel any better about it."

"How do you know?"

"Kyle, we have to work together. I can do that—but if

you can't, maybe you should strongly consider a transfer."

He met her gaze. "You'd like me to do that, but I'm not going anywhere. I'm hoping we can at least be friends."

"We work together," Phillipa said. "That's it. We'll never be friends."

"All I'm asking for is the chance to explain my actions."

"It doesn't matter anymore," she said shortly.

"What are you afraid to hear?" he challenged. "That maybe you're wrong about me?"

"I'm sure you have work to do, Detective."

"I see. You're gonna hide behind your position." Kyle stood up. "I'll leave."

Phillipa smiled but it didn't quite reach her eyes. "Continue the good work, Detective Rossi."

It irked Kyle every time she was so formal. It felt like her way of putting some distance between them.

If they could just sit down and have a real conversation, he believed they could find a way to be comfortable with one another.

Kyle had a feeling that Phillipa was going to fight him every step of the way. However, finding Helena's killer was the priority. He would deal with his heart later.

When Kyle left her office, Phillipa closed her eyes and whispered, "Why did you have to be on my team? I don't want to keep doing this with you." A tremble shot through her as thoughts of him flooded her head. Memories of their time together. Memories she wanted to erase from her heart.

She finished the rest of the one-on-ones with her staff, then returned her focus to Helena's case.

After some serious digging, Phillipa was able to locate one of her siblings and get her on the phone.

"This is Sergeant Phillipa Stevenson with the Charlotte-Mecklenburg Police Department… I'm trying to find some information on Helena Douglas." She traced a line on the notepad with her finger.

"That was my sister. She died fifteen years ago."

"Fifteen?" The Helena she had known died twelve years ago.

"Yes. She had breast cancer."

Phillipa wrote a series of notes as she asked questions. "I see that she was born in Warner Robbins, Georgia. Did she ever live in Atlanta?"

"No, my parents moved to Savannah after Helena was born. She was living in Birmingham when she died. What is this about?"

"I came across her birth certificate in a case I'm working on."

"Identity theft… People can be so trifling."

"You don't have to worry about anything. I'll note it in my file."

Phillipa hung up.

One thing was for sure. She now had a reason to reopen Helena's case. For the moment, she would hold off on saying anything to Kyle. Phillipa wanted to find more information on his sister-in-law before doing so. But she was finally, maybe, getting somewhere.

That night, Phillipa was struck speechless when she opened the front door to find Kyle on the porch.

"What are you doing here?" she asked.

"I came to talk to you."

"Kyle, I told you…"

"I intend to make sure you understand why I called off our engagement."

Phillipa winced, wishing she didn't have to deal with this now. She folded her arms across her chest. "What makes you think I need to hear this all over again? Or that I'd want to rehash one of the most painful periods of my life?"

She'd left town embarrassed, broken-hearted, and bitter. The pain of his rejection carried over into her relationship with her ex-husband, rendering Phillipa unable to tear down the walls erected around her heart.

"Phillipa, move out of the way and let Kyle come in," her mother said.

"He's leaving," she said, meeting his determined gaze without blinking.

Kyle shifted his eyes to her mother, then took a deep breath before returning to Phillipa's face. "No, I'm not," he responded.

Her father walked over and said, "Hear him out, Phillipa."

She sent Kyle an angry glare before stepping aside to let him enter the house.

They sat down in the living room while her parents retreated to the kitchen. No doubt they would listen to determine if interference was necessary. She was glad that Raya was still upstairs finishing up her homework.

"Say whatever it is you have to say," Phillipa uttered.

"I was scared," Kyle began. "I had doubts about being a good husband—being married, period. Then I had a talk with Pastor McCoy and he convinced me to wait until I was sure. I didn't want to go through with the wedding just to have it end in divorce. Philli... Phillipa, I only wanted to postpone it for a couple of months or so. All you heard was that I wanted to cancel the wedding and you wouldn't listen to anything after that."

She wasn't moved by his explanation. "I've heard all this before. If you felt this way, why wait until a week before the wedding?"

"I didn't want to hurt you... I thought it was just pre-wedding jitters, but they never went away."

"I kept asking you if everything was okay. You never once mentioned you were having second thoughts about getting married. Of all people, you listened to a pastor who had had an affair and whose marriage was in trouble." She looked away from Kyle, instead focusing on the painting on the wall behind him. "You should've been honest with me a lot earlier. You have no idea how much money my parents lost by waiting until the last minute to cancel."

"I do know, and I paid them back every cent. You can ask your parents."

The news of that struck her. "I don't think that's necessary," Phillipa responded. "But thank you for doing that, Kyle."

"I'm not as heartless as you think."

"So, what now?"

"Why did you just leave like that?" he inquired. "I asked to postpone the wedding. I wasn't calling it off permanently."

"Be honest, Kyle. We never would've gotten married," she stated. "The truth is that you really didn't want to be a husband. You were content being my boyfriend. I was the one who wanted to get married, and I gave you an ultimatum."

"It started off like that," he admitted. "But I loved you. We would've gotten married before the year was out—if you hadn't left me."

"It's easy for you to say that twelve years later," she responded with a slight shrug. "I don't even know why we're talking about this now. None of it matters anymore." She rose to her feet. "Dinner is almost ready. You should go."

"Thank you for hearing me out."

"Don't expect this to change anything, Kyle."

"I'd like for us to be friends."

"I'm not feeling friendly toward you," she bit out. "If you want to know the truth… I really wish you'd do me a favor and transfer out of my unit."

He gave her a hard stare. "I worked hard to get there and I'm staying."

"That's fine," Phillipa said. "Just remember that we're coworkers and nothing more. Just do your job—that's all I expect of you."

A glimmer of hurt flashed in his eyes before he turned and walked straight to the door. Kyle left without giving Phillipa another glance.

"Why did you have to be so rude?" Bethany asked a minute later when she joined her daughter.

Instead of responding to her mother, she turned to look at her father. "Dad, why didn't you tell me Kyle paid you back?"

"Would it have made a difference?" Jacob asked.

"I don't know, but it would've been nice to know—it could've kept me from putting my foot in my mouth."

"I tried to bring it up, but you never liked talking about Kyle," her mother interjected. "When you married Gary, I felt it was best just to move on."

"You didn't have the right to withhold that information from me," Phillipa stated. "All this time I believed that you and Dad lost the fees you paid. Now I understand why you wouldn't let me pay you back."

"We were trying to spare your feelings," Bethany said.

Jacob headed toward the dining room. "We can finish discussing this after dinner."

"I'm not hungry," Phillipa stated. "I've lost my appetite. I'm going up to my room, but I'll send Raya down."

Right now, she just wanted to be alone.

Chapter Seven

Kyle sat in his car for about twenty minutes after leaving the Stevenson home. He'd finally had a chance to talk to Phillipa but realized there was nothing he could say or do to change the way she thought of him. He hadn't fought hard enough to get her back all those years ago—he should've gone out to Los Angeles after her.

He remembered the very day he'd gone to see her parents to get Phillipa's address and phone number. It was three months after Helena's death. Amid the tragedy, Kyle realized just how much he missed Phillipa and wanted her in his life. So he decided to go to California. Kyle even figured they would get married as soon as possible. He was willing to stay in Los Angeles if that was what Phillipa wanted. However, his plans were sidelined when her parents informed him of her engagement. News of her upcoming marriage felt like a kick to his gut.

He was too late. Kyle could only blame himself. Initially, he was in a bit of denial. She'd been in Los Angeles for just six months; how could she have met someone and agreed to marry him so quickly? Maybe it was Phillipa's way of trying to hurt him.

The idea of another man being her husband and owning her heart didn't sit well with Kyle. There was a part of him that still wanted to fly to California and whisk her away, but his mother talked him out of it—said he had to face the truth. Phillipa was marrying another man. He'd allowed his fears to consume him, and now she was going to be someone else's wife.

But now she was back and no longer married.

Kyle refused to let thoughts of a reconciliation enter his mind. It was much too soon to think that way. Phillipa wasn't even close to forgiving him. She was still so angry. And he would have to get over that hurdle first.

Seeing her again only served to make Kyle realize just how much he'd missed Phillipa all these years.

The next day, Phillipa found Kyle already at his desk. He was going through a murder book and taking notes. He was so involved in his work that he didn't seem to notice her arrival.

She studied him, poised so straight and tall in his crisp pale blue shirt and dark pants. He was devastatingly handsome. Phillipa quickly crushed that thought as soon as it entered her mind. When he looked up at her, Kyle's brown-eyed gaze made the already warm day sizzle. He acknowledged her presence but didn't try to strike up a conversation.

He was either hyperfocused on his case or he wasn't talking to her after the things she said to him when he'd come by the house. Regardless, relief swept through Phillipa as she made it to her office and closed the door behind her.

As soon as she sat down, she went to work on Helena's case. She reviewed a statement that was made by Paula Johnson, Helena's best friend, after the murder. It was time to have a conversation with her.

Phillipa called the number someone had written down on her statement.

"Accounting. This is Paula Johnson speaking…"

"Miss Johnson, I'm Sergeant Stevenson with the Charlotte-Mecklenburg Police. I'm working on the Helena Rossi case."

There was a pause on the line. "Has there been new information?"

"I'd like to talk to you about Helena. I understand you were a friend of hers."

"I was her *best friend*," Paula stated. "I go to lunch at noon. We can talk then. I'd rather you come here to my office. I don't want to go down to the station."

"That's fine," Phillipa responded. "I'll see you then."

She hung up, wondering why Paula preferred to meet with her at work instead of coming to the precinct, but shrugged it away and left shortly after twelve to meet with the woman.

On arrival, Phillipa silently assessed the petite, thin woman who walked into the reception area of the office. Paula was dressed in a chic bright red pantsuit and heels that didn't look at all comfortable to wear for a full workday. Phillipa searched her memory banks and vaguely recalled seeing her at Jon and Helena's wedding. She had been the maid of honor.

"Sergeant Stevenson, it's very nice to meet you in person," Paula said. "We can talk in my office." While they walked down a long hallway, she added, "Jon had nothing but nice things to say about you." She paused a moment. "I feel like I've seen you before."

"I was at Jon and Helena's wedding. I've known the Rossi family a long time," Phillipa said.

"Oh, yes. Jon did mention that." Paula closed the door to her office, then sat down at her desk. "I was a bit surprised when he told me you were going to be investigating Helena's case. Especially since it happened such a long time ago."

"There's no statute of limitations for murder," she responded.

Paula's smile vanished. "I see." She gestured for Phillipa to sit across from her.

"Tell me about your friendship with Helena," Phillipa said, taking a seat.

"I met her when she first came to work. Helena and I started a week apart in the accounting department here at Hawkins Special Events."

"Where did she tell you she was from?"

"Atlanta, I believe."

"Were you two very close?"

"Yeah, like I told you earlier. She was my best friend. We spent a lot of time together back then...going to the movies, eating out and going to dances." Her smile reappeared. "Helena loved to dance. That's how she met Jon. We were at this club in uptown Charlotte. Although the truth is, I met him first."

"You met Jon first."

"I did, but when I introduced him to Helena...he only had eyes for her." Paula shrugged. "But then, she always had a way about her."

"What do you mean?"

"She was flirty. Helena liked a lot of attention." Paula opened a compact mirror and checked her reflection.

Phillipa was surprised to hear this. The Helena she'd known was quite the opposite. She didn't even like taking photographs. "And was she that way after she and Jon got married?"

"Oh, she still liked being the center of attention, but she didn't go out much after that. Helena got pregnant right away. I suppose she needed to secure her position as Jon's wife. She knew he was going to be in the medical field—that he'd be a heart surgeon. Helena told me that as his wife, she'd have status and financial security."

None of this reconciled with the young woman she recalled. "Can you tell me anything you remember that may have struck you as odd at the time?" Phillipa questioned.

She put her compact away. "There was something… It was when Helena and Jon were getting married. I helped her pack up her apartment two weeks before the wedding. I found a degree in accounting from a college in Miami, but it belonged to someone else. I asked Helena about it—she got really upset with me." Paula shook her head. "You should've seen the way she snatched it out of my hands. She then told me that it belonged to some close relative who'd passed away. Helena said it was all she had left of the woman. Now that I think about it, I never saw one for her. Helena put on her job application that she'd earned a degree in accounting." She gave a slight shrug. "I don't know if she really had one or not."

Paula held out her hand as if admiring her manicured fingernails. "Some people lie about stuff like that. All

I know is that I earned mine—it's hanging right over there." She pointed to a frame on the wall.

"Do you think she lied about having a degree?" Phillipa asked.

"No. I'm just saying there are people who do."

"You also stated that you weren't sure that she had one."

"That's the truth," Paula responded. "I don't know for sure."

"Why did you find her behavior so odd at that time?"

"Because of the way she freaked out when I found that degree. I'd never seen Helena act like that. That's all I'm saying."

"Do you happen to remember the name that was on the document?"

"I think it might have been Clara, but I'm not really sure," Paula responded. "Is that important?"

Phillipa found it a bit strange that Helena would have in her possession a degree belonging to someone else. But if it belonged to a deceased relative, it made sense. "Is there anything you can tell me about the days leading up to Helena's disappearance?" she asked.

Paula nodded. "Yeah, she was different."

"In what way?"

"Helena was always nice, but she started to change toward the end. She seemed kind of short-tempered and worried. I was concerned that she'd started abusing drugs. She was just so different."

"As her friend—"

"Her *best* friend," Paula interjected.

"Did you try to talk to her about it?"

"I did, but Helena would just tell me that nothing was going on. She began shutting me out." Paula released a sigh. "I considered going to Jon because I was so concerned about her at the time, but I didn't want to interfere with their marriage. I will say that her death has been terribly hard on him."

Phillipa nodded in understanding.

"Sergeant Stevenson, where exactly are you with this investigation?"

That wasn't something Phillipa could go into. "I thank you for your time, Miss Johnson." She rose to her feet. "I must get back to the precinct."

"You didn't answer my question."

"I'm sorry, but I'm only at liberty to discuss this case with Jon. Again, thank you for your help."

"I'm sure you can find your way out," Paula said in a snippy voice.

Phillipa bit back a grin. "Enjoy the rest of your day."

As soon as she returned to the precinct, Phillipa stopped by Kyle's desk. "I just met Paula. Come to my office when you have a minute. I'd like to know more about her."

"I can come now," he said, rising to his feet.

Once they were behind closed doors, he said, "All I really know is that I've never trusted the woman. According to my mom, Paula chased after Jon even before he married Helena. She was always stopping by my parents' house to see him for one reason or another."

"When I asked about Helena, Paula described her as flirty and attention seeking."

"You know that's not true."

"I didn't think it was, but I didn't know your sister-in-law that well."

"Those characteristics fit Paula to a T," Kyle uttered. "You should see the way she's always trying to insert herself in Jon's life. My mother lives with him, takes care of the house and the girls. It's been twelve years and Paula is still showing up with meals. She's always trying to make plans for my brother and the girls. I keep telling Jon that Paula has ideas about being his next wife. I'm not about to let that happen because she doesn't love him—it's his money she's after."

Helena mentally filed that away for later. "Paula insinuated that Helena may have started taking drugs. She based this on her actions before her death."

He shook his head. "She was pregnant. Besides, there weren't any found in her body at the time of the autopsy."

"I don't think Paula knew about the baby," Phillipa said.

"I told Jon it was best that he keep that bit of information within the family," Kyle responded.

"I agree." She paused a moment before saying, "And speaking of, I need to tell you something, but I want it kept just between us. At least for now."

"Okay. What is it?"

"I told you that Helena's birth certificate was fake. I was right, Kyle. The real Helena died three years before your sister-in-law."

Kyle eyed her in disbelief. "Identity theft...? Helena..."

"Looks that way," Phillipa said. "We just have to find out why."

He looked as if he was searching for words.

"I'm struggling with it myself," she said, meeting his eyes. "I'm thinking we might find the answer in her belongings, or at least some clues to her real identity."

"Jon put all her stuff in a storage unit," he announced.

"He didn't want to get rid of anything. I guess it's a good thing he didn't."

"Do you think he'll let me go through her boxes?" Phillipa asked. "Without a lot of questions?"

"Let me handle my brother. Is this enough to reopen Helena's case?"

Phillipa nodded. "It certainly is. We have to find out exactly who Jon married."

"I'll call Jon right now," Kyle said as he pulled out his phone and walked out into the hallway.

He was reeling from what Phillipa had just told him and needed to step away. After he hung up with his brother a couple minutes later, he walked back into the office. "He's fine with us going to the storage unit. I told him we'd come by to pick up the key."

"*We*, as in you and I?" Phillipa asked.

"I think he'd be more suspicious if it was just you. When he wanted to know why, I told him that I'd like to see if she left anything behind that would help you with the investigation."

He couldn't read her expression. Phillipa was smiling, but he noted that her smile did not quite reach her eyes. "I've given it some thought, and I decided you'd be the best person to assist me in this investigation."

He wasn't expecting that. "Thank you."

He looked around the office, trying to avoid her gaze. Phillipa seemed to have gotten moved in and settled. He glimpsed the many awards and accolades she'd received throughout her career. She had thrown him completely off guard and he had to mentally shake himself to keep from staring.

He eventually nodded succinctly, saying, "Meet you

outside," then left the room and walked past several open workspaces to get to his desk.

Kyle retrieved his duty weapon, which was kept locked in a drawer while he was working. He met Phillipa outside by the detective cruiser assigned to him.

"I figured I'd drive," he said as he held open the front passenger side door.

"Do you think Jon will be okay with us taking items we find into evidence?" she inquired.

"I'm sure he won't mind," Kyle said. "All her stuff is just sitting in storage."

"Would you mind stopping at Cook-Out? I've been wanting one of their burgers since moving back, and I skipped lunch."

"You mean you haven't had one?"

"I haven't," she responded with a grin. "I've been craving a single hamburger with everything but cheese."

"But add bacon," Kyle finished for her.

"You remembered?"

"It's imprinted on my memory. You used to get so mad at me when I forgot to tell them that you didn't want cheese."

Phillipa surprised him by laughing. "I was horrible."

"I wouldn't say that. You just wanted what you wanted—I understood."

"Do they still serve Coke floats?"

"They do," Kyle responded.

Phillipa looked over at him. "Do you still get the onion rings and hush puppies as your sides?"

"Yeah. Always."

"I guess some things just don't change."

Kyle broke into a grin.

As they neared Jon's house after getting their take-out, Phillipa stared out the window. "I hope we'll find something that will give us a clue to Helena's real identity. And offer some insight as to why she was using another person's name."

"Me, too."

She stayed in the car to finish her hamburger as he approached the door, but the women waved at each other when his mother answered it.

Kyle accepted the key she held out to him.

"Thanks, Mom."

"It's good seeing you two together," Amelie said.

"We're at work—not on a date," Kyle said.

His mother quirked a brow. "The Lord works in mysterious ways."

He smiled. "I'll see you later."

Kyle walked back to the car and got inside. He was glad to be going with Phillipa to the storage unit. He had so many questions swirling around in his head. He'd never expected that reopening Helena's case would prompt another mystery.

Fifteen minutes later, they arrived at their destination. He drove through the iron gates surrounding the storage facility and they got out of the car.

"It's B-230," Kyle said. He had no idea what to expect or what they'd find.

"Here's to hoping we find answers and not more questions," Phillipa said.

Nodding, Kyle responded, "I couldn't have said that better myself."

Chapter Eight

They were alone in the midsize storage unit, surrounded by rows of cardboard boxes and large clear containers.

"What are you doing?" Phillipa asked as Kyle reached toward her face.

"You have something in your hair." He retrieved what looked like a piece of a feather from a curly tendril.

"Oh," she uttered. "Thanks."

His gorgeous brown eyes were as mesmerizing as ever as he flashed her one of his trademark grins. "You're welcome."

Phillipa hated that she could still go weak in the knees around Kyle. The last thing she wanted was to give him the idea that this little truce between them was going to lead to something more.

After clearing her throat softly, she said, "You can start with the boxes on the right. I'll look through these."

"What are we looking for?"

"Anything that will give us a glimpse into Helena's life before she came to Charlotte."

"I'll start with the older boxes first," Kyle said. "My

sister-in-law was organized. She put dates on everything."

"That will help to sort things out for us," Phillipa
responded.

As they worked toward a common goal, she relaxed
and stifled her bitter feelings toward Kyle.

Phillipa quickly found an old photo album with photographs of Helena as a child. Many of the pictures of
her were taken at a beach. Another album showed her
life as a senior in high school and her college years. She
noted Helena was often in the company of two other
girls during that time in her life.

Phillipa put the albums to the side. She planned on
taking them with her.

"You find anything?" Kyle asked.

"Photographs," she responded. "Looks like she spent
a lot of time at the beach when she was growing up."

"That makes sense. Helena always loved the beach.
She used to say that the beaches in Miami were her favorite."

"Maybe her family used to vacation there," Phillipa suggested. "Did you happen across any degrees or
transcripts? Paula said that Helena had one that didn't
belong to her. She thinks the first name might have
been Clara."

"Not yet."

Phillipa went through another box but didn't find
anything she considered relevant to Helena's case.

"How's your search going?" she asked.

"Haven't really found anything," Kyle responded. "I
still have a few other boxes to go through."

Phillipa sat there with the photo albums on her lap.
She hoped they would prove to be an important piece of

the puzzle. She opened the one on top and took out a photograph of Helena with the same two women from high school. This time, they were dressed in caps and gowns.

"Kyle, they graduated from the University of Miami," Phillipa said. *This is something.* "We need a name though."

She continued looking, checking box after box for clues to Helena's real identity.

"Jon never went through her stuff?" Phillipa inquired.

"I don't think so," Kyle replied. "She must have kept this hidden during their marriage. And after… I think it was just too painful for him. My parents packed up her things for him and my dad put them here in storage."

"I was sad to hear when your father passed," she said. "He was a really good man."

He nodded. "He was that. Helena hadn't even been gone a good six months when we had to deal with his death."

"I can't imagine," Phillipa murmured as she pulled a stack of papers out of a cardboard box marked Documents. She set the photo albums off to the side so she could focus on the papers.

Kyle searched through box after box but kept coming up with nothing. The last box was labeled School Memories. He opened it and saw a degree in a cardboard frame.

"I found it," he said. "It belongs to a Clara Davis, and it's from the University of Miami. There's also a high school diploma and transcript in here, too. Same name. Clara Davis."

Phillipa glanced over her shoulder. "Is there anything else? A birth certificate maybe?"

"Nothing that'll help us. Wait…" Kyle said. "There are several old newspapers in here. *The Miami Herald.* Looks like they're all from 2006."

"Bring them with us," Phillipa stated. "They might be useful."

They put a box containing the newspapers and photo albums in the back seat.

"Do you think Clara Davis and Helena are the same person?" he asked when they were back in the car.

"I'm beginning to believe it's very possible. We don't have another name to go on. We just need to know why she changed her name."

"Maybe she was in witness protection."

Phillipa looked at Kyle. "I thought about that, too. I'll put a call in with the US Marshals when I get back to the station. Don't know how much I'll be able to get out of them, but I do have a friend with the agency. Maybe she can find out something for me."

She nodded. "Kyle, thanks for your help."

"I'm happy to assist."

Her face didn't give anything away as she asked, "Why?"

"Because there was a time when we were partners. I miss it."

"Sometimes I do, too," Phillipa said. "Then I remind myself that it doesn't do any good to live in the past."

Kyle bit back a retort. It was probably best to let the comment go without a response.

He had gotten a smile out of her.

It would have to be enough.

Back at the office, Phillipa opened the album containing the high school and college photographs. On the back of one was written:

Clara, Myra, Kelsey
Friends Forever!

"Okay, I'm convinced that Helena and Clara are the same person," she said when Kyle walked into her office. She handed him the photo. "There's no mention of the name Helena anywhere before 2006. I think we should look for a birth certificate for Clara Davis."

"I really think we should hold off saying anything to Jon," Kyle responded. "At least until we find out the reason Helena was lying about her real identity. I can't deny that I find this troubling."

"I'm inclined to agree with you. I did put in a call to the Marshals. I'm waiting for a call back."

While Kyle went to his desk to take an incoming phone call, Phillipa scanned the newspaper articles. One immediately caught her attention.

When he was done, Kyle returned to her office.

Without looking up, she said, "You won't believe this… Two girls went missing in Miami. Clara Davis and Myra Rowland."

"Clara…" Kyle uttered.

Phillipa nodded. "I'm beginning to understand why she changed her name." She put the newspapers in order by date, and started reading the next one. "There was a big search for the girls."

Phillipa continued reading, then said, "Myra's body was found just outside of Miami. They found her two weeks later."

"Any mention of Clara?"

"During that time, she was still considered missing," Phillipa replied. "According to this article, Clara's mother said that the girls had been running around with a known drug dealer and his crew. She believes he's responsible for what happened to Myra and her daughter."

Kyle shook his head in confusion. "I can't imagine Helena hanging around someone like that."

"I can't either."

Phillipa found another article. "Kyle, according to this, Clara's decomposed body was found a few weeks after they found Myra's but get this…her body was found near Atlanta. *She's dead.*"

Kyle shook his head. "We know that can't be…especially if she and Helena are the same person."

Phillipa nodded. "Exactly. The pictures I found are of Clara and two girls. Clara and the other girl, Kelsey, resemble each other enough to be related."

"Are you thinking that the body found was Kelsey's?"

"Could've been, but none of the articles mention that she was missing. In fact, she was supposedly interviewed by Miami PD."

"So we now have two other bodies…"

"What's interesting is that Myra was shot in the chest. Same as Helena. This other girl who's supposed to be Clara was shot in the head."

"Are you thinking that maybe Myra and Helena were killed by the same person?" he asked.

"It makes sense, don't you think?"

"It's a possibility, I guess," Kyle stated. "But if Clara and Helena are the same person, then who does the other body belong to?"

"That's what we have to find out," Phillipa said. "Did you happen to bring the yearbooks with you?"

"I did," Kyle replied.

They went through the North Miami High School yearbook.

She pointed to a picture. "Kelsey Brown…that's the third girl."

"Okay, great," he said. "Now, how do we find her?"

"Let's start with her social media," Phillipa stated. "If we can't find her there, we'll try her family."

"Or I can take social media while you try to locate her family," he offered. "That might help us find her faster."

"Sure. That's fine."

While she was grateful for his assistance, another worry came to her. "Make sure you're not neglecting your other cases, Kyle."

"I'm not," he said. "You should know me better than that. I learned a long time ago how to multitask."

Two hours later, Kyle was back in her office. "I found a few Kelsey Browns on social media."

"Kelsey's parents are still at the same address they lived at when she was in high school," Phillipa said while picking up the telephone receiver.

Kyle sat down across from her. Their eyes met and held.

Phillipa released a soft sigh, though she wasn't sure if it was one of contentment or apprehension.

"Hello, I'm trying to reach Kelsey Brown," she said when a woman picked up.

"This is her mother. I'm afraid she doesn't live in Miami anymore. May I ask who's calling, please?"

"My name is Sergeant Phillipa Stevenson. I'm with the Charlotte-Mecklenburg Police Department. I'd really like to speak with your daughter. It's very important."

She placed the call on speaker so Kyle could hear.

"Can you tell me what this is about? Is Kelsey in trouble?"

"No, she isn't. All I can say is that this is about two of her friends. Clara Davis and Myra Rowland."

"I remember them… It's a shame what happened. They were sweet girls."

"Could you please give my number to Kelsey?" Phillipa asked. "I'd really like to speak with her."

"I don't understand what this has to do with you in Charlotte. Those girls weren't found there."

"I'm just following up on a lead, ma'am."

The woman sighed. "Well, Kelsey lives in Virginia now. Can't you leave her out of this?"

"She's not in any trouble, I assure you. We just want to speak with her. There may not be anything she can tell us, but I have to try."

"I'll give her your message and ask her to call you. It'll be up to her whether you hear back."

"Thank you, Mrs. Brown. I really appreciate this."

"Do you think you'll hear from Kelsey?" Kyle asked after she hung up.

"I really don't know. I doubt there's much she can really tell me anyway, but I still want to talk to her."

"Are you going to tell her about Helena?"

"No," Phillipa said. "I don't plan to. I want to know what Kelsey knows."

"Would you let me know if you hear from her?" he asked on his way out of the office. "I'm going to see to some other casework."

"Sure."

An hour later, the phone rang. She answered it. "Sergeant Stevenson speaking…"

"This is Kelsey Brown. My mother said you wanted to talk to me." Her voice was shaky. She was nervous.

"Yes, I do. Thanks so much for calling me back."

"What is this about?" she asked.

"What can you tell me about Myra Rowland and Clara Davis's relationship?"

"They were friends. We were always together and were very close. People used to call us the Three Musketeers." She paused a moment, then said, "When they died, I felt like part of me died with them."

Her heart went out to Kelsey. "I understand Clara was cremated. Was there a memorial or service for her?"

"There was a memorial service at their church," Kelsey said. "Her father had her cremated in Atlanta. He and his brother owned a funeral home there—Davis Funeral Home."

Phillipa jotted down notes as they talked.

"I don't suppose you can tell me what all this is about?" Kelsey asked.

"We're working with Miami and Georgia homicide detectives by following up on some leads. Both Myra and Clara's deaths remain unsolved."

"I guess you're trying to find the people responsible?"

She found it interesting that Kelsey said *people* instead of *person*. "Yes, we would like to be able to close these cases and get justice for your friends. I noticed you said 'people.' Is there a reason you believe it was more than one person?"

"I'm not sure why I said that… Honestly, I don't think I can be of much help, Sergeant Stevenson. I wasn't with them the day they disappeared. I don't even like to think about it. If I had been… I might have ended up dead, too."

"One last question," Phillipa said. "Have you ever heard the name Helena Douglas or Helena Rossi?"

"No, I haven't."

"Thank you for calling me back."

"You're welcome."

"Oh, one more thing," Phillipa added. "Is Clara's mother still in Miami?" she asked.

"She died not too long after Clara," Kelsey responded. "I've heard that people can die from a broken heart. It sure seems like she did."

At the end of the call, Phillipa pushed away from her desk and got up. She stood in the doorway and gestured for Kyle to join her. "I just spoke to Kelsey Brown."

He got up and headed toward her. "She actually called you."

"I didn't think I'd hear from her at all," Phillipa responded as when he entered her office and sat down.

She took her seat behind her desk.

"Kelsey sounded scared and very nervous during our conversation." Phillipa recapped it, referring to the notes she'd taken. "Kelsey may have a point when she said if she'd been with Myra and Clara, she might have ended up dead, too."

"I guess we can cross her off the witness list."

"You know what…leave her on it for now," Phillipa said.

"Why do you want to do that?" Kyle inquired.

"Until we can rule them completely out, everyone will be kept on our witness list, unless we have to move them to the suspect list," Phillipa responded.

"I feel like we're pulling at straws."

She agreed. "Helena's life was far more complicated than anyone ever knew."

Kyle nodded. "Maybe it was her desire for a simple life that ended up getting her killed."

Chapter Nine

The next afternoon, Phillipa rode with Kyle to return the storage unit key to Jon's place. She wanted to get some fresh air and just take a break from sitting in her office all day long. She normally didn't leave the precinct during the day, not even for lunch.

It was actually Kyle's suggestion for Phillipa to get out of her office for a couple of hours. He told her that his mother was asking to see her. She could never refuse Amelie Rossi anything. Phillipa loved her almost as much as she loved her own mother.

When they arrived, Amelie met her at the door. The two women embraced.

"I missed you so much."

"I missed you, too, Miss Amelie. I'm sorry I didn't stay in contact with you…"

"Honey, I understood. You'd started a new life, but you're here now. I expect I'll be seeing you from time to time."

"Yes, ma'am. You sure will," she promised. Despite that she was still keeping Kyle at arm's length, they did work together and were on a case together. There was no need to distance herself from Amelie.

"When Kyle told me you were coming, I made lunch."

"You didn't have to go through all this trouble."

"Wasn't no trouble at all," Amelie responded.

Phillipa was only mildly surprised when Paula showed up at Jon's house with food a short time later. Kyle was right—she was definitely trying to insert herself into his life.

She sashayed in wearing a cute royal blue suit and those spike heels she seemed to love shortly after Jon arrived home for lunch. Her cropped hair was styled to complement her heart-shaped face.

"Oh… I didn't know you'd be here," she stammered when she saw Phillipa. "Or you, Kyle…"

He smiled at Paula. "What did I tell you?" he whispered when she'd turned away.

"Maybe if you'd pick up the phone and call sometime, you'd know," Amelie uttered as the other woman bustled about the kitchen. "Paula, we appreciate you taking the time to cook, but I prepare the meals around here. Been doing so for the past twelve years."

Paula glared at the woman before pasting on a fake smile. "Mrs. Rossi, I know you've got your hands full with the girls and everything. I just thought I'd help a little."

Phillipa knew Amelie Rossi was nobody to play with. There wasn't an opinion she held that she hesitated to share. She either liked you or she didn't. Amelie was never lukewarm when it came to how she felt about people.

Hands on her hips, Amelie said, "If it's help I'm needing, I'll call you and tell you so."

Jon and Kyle exchanged amused looks.

Paula glanced at Jon as if she expected him to come to her defense. When he didn't, she said, "Yes, ma'am. I was only trying to lighten your load."

She was about to take a seat when Amelie said, "Jon has business to discuss, so you don't need to wait around. Thank you again for the food."

"I'll give you a call later," she told Jon before stalking out of the house.

"I can't stand that woman," Amelie uttered. "Jon, I don't know why you don't come out and tell her that she's wasting her time on you."

"I told him the same thing," Kyle said.

Jon shrugged. "She's trying to be a friend. That's all."

"You don't believe that any more than I do," Kyle said.

"That's all she can ever be to me," Jon responded.

"You need to tell her that," his mother stated.

"I have."

"Maybe you need to say it a little louder," Kyle suggested.

Amelie turned her attention to him and Phillipa. "Have you two settled your differences?"

Phillipa glanced over at Kyle, then said, "Yes, we have." Settled enough to find justice for Helena anyway. She knew they had to put the past aside and work together.

"Good to hear."

She heard voices outside.

"My girls are home," Jon announced. "I'm glad you're here, Phillipa. I'd like them to meet you."

When the twins entered the house, he called them into the dining room.

"Y'all just in time to eat with us," Amelie interjected before he made the introductions.

Phillipa took an instant liking to the girls. They seemed to feel the same way about her as they engaged her in conversation while they ate.

She glanced over at Kyle, who had been silent during their interchange, and smiled.

He smiled back.

"I'll have to introduce you to my daughter. She's a bit younger than you are though. She's almost eleven."

"That doesn't matter if she's cool," Joi said. "My best friend is twelve. She lives next door."

Her sister, Toya, finished off her water before asking, "Can we meet her soon?"

"Phillipa and I will work out a playdate," Jon said, and she nodded in agreement.

Kyle and Phillipa said their goodbyes and left right after they finished eating.

When they walked back into the precinct, she headed straight to her office. "Thank you for getting me out of here for a bit. I have to go to a meeting now, but I'll check in with you later."

Phillipa needed a moment to regroup and get back into her supervisor role. She'd enjoyed lunch with Kyle and his family. It brought back unexpected but wonderful memories of other lunches and dinners with the Rossi's.

She wasn't afraid of the memories resurfacing; it was letting down her guard even a little that frightened her. Phillipa had to keep her focus on Helena's case—she didn't want it shifting to Kyle or the emotions she struggled to keep at bay.

* * *

Her steps were brisk and abrupt, almost as if Phillipa couldn't wait to get away from him. Kyle reminded himself that no matter their history, she was still a bit of a mystery to him. One he wasn't sure he should want to explore.

Phillipa had changed over the years. He still caught glimpses of the woman he had fallen in love with, but now there was a hardness to her as well that hadn't been there years ago.

It bothered Kyle because he knew he was the cause of it.

Yet he also knew he needed to place his full attention on another cold case he'd been working on. He'd just gotten a new lead from a ballistics report.

He couldn't afford to let Phillipa become a distraction.

Kyle opened a file and read over his notes before adding additional information on ballistics and other trace evidence.

Bryant rolled his chair over to Kyle's desk. "I need to run something by you. I'm working on the Amy Rhoads case. Remember she was the young woman killed in the drug store along with three other employees."

"She's the one whose brother had testified against some gangbanger, right?"

"Yep. The detective who performed the initial investigation theorized that it was a random robbery-turned-homicide. I don't agree," Bryant said. "My gut tells me that Amy was the intended victim. The others were just in the wrong place at the wrong time."

"Why do you say that?" Kyle asked.

"She was the only one with multiple stab wounds."

"If I remember correctly, the Black kid was tortured and beaten to death. The other two vics were shot."

"The gang Amy's brother testified against…they're known for spouting racist rhetoric."

"Follow your gut and see where it leads you," Kyle said. It was common for them to bounce cases off each other. He knew Bryant would be there when he needed the same for one of his cases.

Bryant went back to his desk, leaving him to continue working his own case.

Kyle looked up. He could see into Phillipa's office. She was squeezing a stress ball as she stared at whatever was displayed on her monitor.

He turned his attention back to his own computer screen. Working this close to Phillipa wasn't as easy as he'd initially thought it would be. Still, he didn't regret bringing her onboard.

He was still drawn to her despite maintaining his professionalism in the office.

She'd already made it clear that the most he would hope for was a working relationship with her. However, Kyle yearned for the friendship that once came so easy for them. He didn't care for walking gently around as if stepping on eggshells.

Something was going to have to change between them.

Phillipa escaped into a conference room. But it was the way Kyle stood a few yards away at a copier, his head cocked to one side, an air of confidence about him, that drew her like a moth to a flame.

She checked her watch. Her meeting wasn't scheduled to start for another ten minutes. She needed that time to regain her senses.

Phillipa cast her gaze outside the window, where a light breeze stirred the trees. She always loved this time of year.

She heard the door open and close. Phillipa's thoughts snapped back to the present as supervisors from other departments slowly filled the room. Phillipa tried to turn her attention to the meeting agenda, but reluctantly, her thoughts traveled back to Kyle. A strange sensation overtook her.

Kyle had turned and was watching her. He seemed to be looking inside her soul, which prompted Phillipa to break eye contact with him.

It was ridiculous, the kind of tension his very presence wrought inside her. She was extremely aware of Kyle, when all she wanted was to look at him as just another employee.

Ever since Phillipa made the decision to come home, she'd had a feeling her life was going to change. She just wasn't sure if it was for better or worse. She was tired of the shadows of loneliness that often tried to overtake her.

Not that she was looking to have a relationship with Kyle. Phillipa really didn't want to deal with problems on the job that a personal liaison could bring. Her only priorities were her daughter and thriving in her new position.

She added Helena's case to that list.

"How do you like being back in Charlotte?" Jon asked. He'd called and invited Phillipa to meet him for lunch at the hospital two days later.

"It's good to be home," Phillipa responded. "Raya seems to be adjusting well. Initially, she was very resistant to relocating... Jon, she threw the biggest fit. But now she's a different girl. She has friends and she likes the school. I love seeing her happy."

"That's great. I can't wait for her to meet my daughters."

"We have to plan something soon," Phillipa said. "Raya is looking forward to meeting them as well."

"My brother's not a bad guy."

She gave him a wry smile. "I know."

"You should know that he still loves you, Philli. That's never changed."

"We had our moment," she said. "Twelve years ago. We're finally in a space where we can work together without so much tension between us. It's best all-around if we don't revisit the past. There's no need to."

"Even if it's the key to your future?"

She didn't respond.

Phillipa glanced up to see Paula heading their way. She couldn't help but wonder if the woman ever worked a full day. According to Amelie and Kyle, not a day went by when she wasn't showing up for one reason or another.

"Jon, I thought I'd surprise you for lunch," she said. "I guess I should've called you first."

"You remember Sergeant Stevenson, don't you?" he asked.

"I do," Paula uttered, her tone suddenly frosty. "I didn't expect to see you here with Jon."

"So I gathered," Phillipa responded.

Paula sat down with them without preamble. "Jon, I

have tickets to see the Elements for next Friday. They're center stage, second row. VIP…"

"I have two surgeries scheduled that day," Jon said. "You should've talked to me first before you spent the money on them."

"I wanted to surprise you," Paula responded.

"I'm sorry," he said regretfully, "but I won't be able to go."

"Aren't your surgeries usually in the mornings?" she asked.

"I have one that morning and the other in the afternoon. I'm also on call next weekend."

Phillipa pushed away from the table, feeling she was interrupting by now. "I should get back to work. It's always nice seeing you, Jon."

She nodded at them both and left the cafeteria.

"Sergeant Stevenson…"

She turned around to face Paula, who had caught up with her. "What is it?"

"I hope you don't have designs on Jon because it's not gonna work. I heard you were engaged to Kyle once. If you're thinking you can use his brother to get back at him…"

"Before you make a complete fool of yourself, let me stop you," Phillipa said. "Jon and I are friends. I'm investigating his wife's case, so we're going to be spending time together."

"I was just—"

"Quit while you're ahead, Miss Johnson." Phillipa walked off without giving Paula an opportunity to respond.

The woman was ruthless. And seemed to have no shame.

"I just left Jon," Phillipa said to Kyle when she re-turned to the precinct. "I ran into Paula while I was there. She had the nerve to confront me about your brother."

"Really?"

She nodded. "She actually dared to accuse me of using your brother to get back at you."

Kyle burst into laughter.

Phillipa laughed with him. "That woman is some-thing else."

"Nothing good," he responded.

Chapter Ten

Kyle shifted in his seat to keep from falling asleep. He'd been at the precinct going on ten hours now. The last four hours were spent in a training session. It didn't help that the facilitator was talking in a monotone voice, which bored him senseless.

He rose to his feet and eased out of the room. Hopefully moving around a bit could wake him up some.

Kyle stopped in a nearby restroom to pat cold water on his face before navigating to the break room. He grabbed a soda and energy bar.

"Kyle?"

He turned around to find Phillipa standing in the doorway.

"Taking a break?" she inquired.

"Yeah, I needed one."

Despite the tense moments with her, Kyle felt as if an invisible thread was pulling them together. When he looked from her dark brown eyes down to her perfectly shaped lips, he suddenly felt the urge to kiss her.

"Hey, are you okay?"

Kyle nodded. "I just came in here to get something

to drink and move around. I should get back to the training room."

He brushed past her.

The soda and energy bar gave Kyle exactly what he needed to make it through the last hour of the class. He made a mental note to never come to work early on a day he had a training session.

Phillipa was still heavy on Kyle's mind by the time he made it home. He had been putting forth a valiant effort to keep her out of his thoughts, but it was proving much harder than he'd thought it would to only see her as his supervisor.

He could better understand Phillipa's reluctance to let him get close to her, especially after all they'd shared… all the memories of the time they'd spent together. He had to keep his thoughts under control.

Kyle wondered if Phillipa was having the same struggles. A part of him hoped so—it helped him to think they had this in common.

The next day, Phillipa spent her morning going over her notes on Helena, making sure she hadn't missed anything.

It was almost eleven when a US marshal finally returned her call.

Fifteen minutes later, Phillipa hung up her phone, then got up and walked to Kyle's desk. "The Marshals don't have a Clara Davis or a Helena Douglas in the witness protection program."

"So much for that theory," Kyle responded. "I read through those articles surrounding her and Myra's disappearance. I hope you don't mind that I called to speak to the detective who initially handled the case. He said

they believed a drug dealer called Savage was responsible for the girls' deaths, but they couldn't arrest him
because he had a solid alibi when they disappeared. He
was at the hospital. His *girlfriend* was giving birth to
his child. Savage was murdered a few months later by
an unknown assailant."

Phillipa felt a bit irritated that Kyle had done that
without consulting her but understood his yearning to
help. She decided not to make an issue of it, but she
planned to call the detective to follow up and present
her theory on Helena's double life. "If Savage is the one
who killed Myra, then why would he take Clara all the
way to Atlanta?"

"Maybe she ran away, and Savage found her there,"
he offered. "Maybe she was a witness to what happened
and that's why she was murdered."

She silently considered his idea. "Didn't the article
say that the body found in Atlanta was badly decomposed?" Phillipa asked.

"Yeah."

"The body was found wearing the same clothes from
when Clara went missing. It was Clara's father who
identified the remains."

"None of this is making sense," Kyle said. "I have
more questions now than I had before."

"So do I," Phillipa murmured.

"Helena was cremated as well. I don't know how
Jon will feel about it, but we can still get DNA from
her bone fragments and teeth," Kyle stated. "We just
need to find out where Clara's ashes are located. Then
maybe we can prove that those ashes don't belong to
the real Clara."

"I don't think we're going to find those ashes," she said. "I'm sure they've vanished like a mirage."

"You're probably right."

Still, Phillipa wasn't ready to give up on the idea of analyzing the remains. "We'll keep making calls and see what comes up. But even if we can't identify the other body, we can use DNA to prove that Helena and Clara are the same person."

"What reason would we give my brother to get his permission to analyze Helena's remains?" Kyle asked.

"We don't have one that wouldn't arouse his suspicions." Phillipa swiped an escaping tendril from her face. "For now, I'll hold off on that unless there's no other way to solve this case."

After work, Phillipa met her mother at Mert's Heart and Soul, located on College Street, for dinner. Her father and Raya were attending the Father-Daughter Dance at her school.

"I love this place," she said, taking a seat at a table near the window. "It's always been one of my favorite restaurants."

"The food here is great," Bethany responded. "Especially the soul rolls."

"I missed those little egg rolls filled with black-eyed peas, rice, collard greens and diced chicken. They are so delicious with that spicy honey mustard sauce."

Grinning, her mother said, "Let's order some."

Phillipa nodded as she scanned the menu. "Okay, we're having the soul rolls for starters. For my main entrée, I'll get the salmon cakes." Laying the menu on the table, she said, "I'm glad you suggested this, Mom. It's the perfect way to end a busy workday."

Bethany looked across the room. "Hey, isn't that Kyle over there?"

Phillipa stole a peek over her shoulder.

"Yeah," she responded as casually as she could manage, turning back to face her mother. "Did you tell him we were coming here?"

"I haven't spoken to Kyle," Bethany stated. "Honestly, Phillipa, do you really think I'd do something like that without mentioning it to you?"

"No, I don't. It's just that he's the last person I'd expect to run into here of all places. He was never a huge fan of Mert's. At least that's what he used to say when we were together."

After their server came to take their order, the thought that he had followed her entered Phillipa's mind, but she quickly chased it away. Kyle would never do something like that, would he?

"Did you mention that you were coming here for dinner?" Bethany asked. "Maybe he overheard you talking to me."

Phillipa shook her head. "I'm sure this is just a coincidence. I don't think he knows we're here. He hasn't looked this way once."

"Looks like he might actually be working," Bethany said. "That looks like a file of some sort."

Phillipa watched him for a moment. He was focused on whatever he was reading. She was impressed by his dedication.

"So, how are things going with him?" Bethany asked in a whisper that somehow managed to carry over the noisy din of the crowded dining hall.

"Much better than I ever expected," she responded. "I think we're finding our rhythm."

"That's wonderful to hear."

"But it's also challenging," Phillipa said. "Mom, I can't seem to keep him out of my mind."

"You still care for him, honey. I can see it all over your face."

"I don't want to feel that way about Kyle. He hurt me terribly."

"You have to lay the past to rest."

"I can't," Phillipa responded. "I've tried, Mom. I can't do it. The pain is like a permanent fixture in my heart. I'm doing everything I can to learn to live with it."

"The other option is to forgive and let go of the pain. With the Lord's help, you can let all that go," Bethany said. "Can you say that you've truly done that?"

"He broke my heart." She'd been so excited about the wedding, so sure of them—but he hadn't. Everything had ended so suddenly.

"Honey, Kyle was having some doubts and he came to you to talk about them. You were the one who ended the relationship."

"Because I truly believed that's where we were heading," Phillipa said. "I just didn't want to delay what I thought was inevitable."

"You panicked," Bethany stated. "And you ran away."

Had she panicked? "I didn't know what else to do."

"You could've stayed and fought for your relationship."

She glanced over at the table where Kyle sat. His attention was glued to the file in his hand.

"I suppose so," Phillipa said after a moment. "I just didn't think there was anything left to fight for."

Kyle looked up just as his friend approached the table.

"Did you see Phillipa?" Bryant asked as he sat down. He put away his file. "See her where?"

"She's up front with someone. I think it's her mother." Kyle peeked around Bryant. "I was focused on work."

"You two have been quite chummy lately."

"We're working a case together."

"You never know what might come out of it," Bryant said. "Maybe old feelings will be rekindled."

"Don't you have some cases to solve? Or a girlfriend to pay attention to?" Kyle asked. "What Phillipa and I had ended a long time ago. Let's leave it in the past."

"I would, but I don't believe it's what you really want."

"What I want doesn't matter. Right now, I want to be able to close Helena's case for Jon and their daughters. That's what's really important."

"I hear you," Bryant said. "But I know how much you loved Phillipa. I'd like to see you win her back. I'm rooting for y'all."

"And I'd like to see you propose to Camellia," Kyle shot back at his friend. "You've kept her waiting long enough. You've been together for what? Five or six years now?"

Picking up the menu, Bryant said, "Okay… I hear you. Mind my own business."

Kyle hadn't expected to run into Phillipa at the restaurant, despite knowing that it was one of her favorite places to dine. If Bryant hadn't said anything, he never would've known she was there. He debated whether to get up and say hello, eventually deciding to wait until he was on his way out. The last time he'd interrupted dinner, Phillipa hadn't been at all happy about it.

He smiled as he observed her enjoying dinner with her mother. Phillipa was all grins and laughter. Kyle loved seeing her like this. The scene reminded him of the way she used to be—wonderful memories all around.

"You ready to order?" Bryant asked.

"Huh?" Kyle glanced up at the server. "I'm sorry. I'll have the grilled salmon, please."

When the server left, he glanced over at Phillipa again. Their gazes met and held.

He gave a nod in greeting.

She smiled in return.

In the office, Phillipa was the ultimate professional. Kyle couldn't help but wonder if she ever let her hair down to have a good time anymore.

The next day, Phillipa stopped by Dillon Park after work before heading home.

The squeals and laughter of the children playing died along with the light of the day. As evening merged into night, the grass was finally given a chance to recover from the footfalls, balls and picnics of the day.

Phillipa walked past trees swaying gently in the wind as falling leaves scurried along the path in front of her. She headed to the gazebo and sat down, staring out at the rose garden. She had come hoping to clear her mind.

Before too long, the tiny hairs at the nape of her neck and along Phillipa's arms stood to attention. Her heart started to race.

Someone was watching her. She could feel the weight of their gaze. Her eyes bounced around, taking in her surroundings and searching past the trees.

Phillipa didn't see anyone.

Was it the person who killed Helena? Or some other unknown threat?

Swallowing her panic, Phillipa stood up, placed her hand on her department-issued firearm and walked to her car, locking the doors as soon as she was safely inside.

There were several cars in the parking lot, their owners scattered around the grounds.

Phillipa continued looking around, searching. When she didn't notice anything out of the norm, she left the park.

Phillipa decided not to mention what had happened to her family, because she didn't want to worry them. Besides, there wasn't much to tell. It could have just been her overactive imagination.

Naw… She was sure someone had been watching her.

Phillipa felt certain she wasn't followed home. She'd checked the rearview mirror more than a few times. This was her main concern—she wanted to make sure her family was safe.

Her father had a high-tech security system installed, and both her parents were skilled with a gun, which gave her some added peace of mind.

She rushed into the house and found her father in his office. Her mother and Raya were in the kitchen getting dinner ready. Phillipa released a soft sigh of relief. They were all safe. For now anyway.

Maybe it was this investigation that had her so rattled...or the fact that whoever was hiding in the shadows knew the truth about Clara Davis and Helena Douglas.

Chapter Eleven

That Sunday Phillipa and her daughter attended church services with her parents. The pastor's sermon was on forgiveness—something she didn't want to hear about. She thought of her ex-husband and wondered if he'd been able to forgive her.

A thread of guilt snaked down her spine as Phillipa considered that she wanted Gary to forgive her, but she was unwilling to forgive Kyle.

I don't want to deal with this right now.

As soon as they walked out of the sanctuary at the end of the service, Raya asked, "Mama, can we go to the park?"

"Sure, if all of your homework is done."

"It is," Raya confirmed.

They went home and changed clothes first.

Phillipa felt a bit hesitant about going back to Dillon Park so soon after the last incident, but she didn't want to disappoint Raya. At any rate, the park seemed different to her today. The sunshine seemed to melt into the laughter of the children running around the grounds, the leaves on the trees as light as the wings of butterflies.

They walked past the gazebo to the lake area.

"Can we rent a boat and go for a ride?" Raya asked.

"I was thinking we should do just that," Phillipa said with a chuckle. She loved spending quality time with her daughter, and she intended to make the most of the afternoon. Tomorrow it was back to work, to long hours and a desk buried underneath a stack of cases, departmental reports and case summaries. But Phillipa was looking forward to next Saturday when they celebrated Raya's birthday.

Fifteen minutes later, she and Raya were in a boat rowing across the lake.

There was a calmness to the water as it met the sun with grace. The two seemed to be entwined in an eternal dance of love.

Smiling, Phillipa eyed the ripples in reflective blues and greens, bringing its own artistic watercolor effect to the willing canvas of their surroundings.

"This is super fun," Raya said.

"I agree," she responded. "This is one of the best days I've had so far. Mostly because I'm spending it with my favorite girl."

"Next time, we should bring Grandma with us. We can have a girls' day."

Phillipa agreed.

After they were done rowing, they spent the next hour on a bike trail around the park. Although she was enjoying her time with Raya, Phillipa was very aware of her surroundings. Thankfully, there were no odd sensations this time around—nothing to indicate she might be in danger.

Maybe it was just my imagination. But deep down, she believed otherwise.

* * *

"Uncle K, let's go to Dillon Park," Joi suggested. "We haven't been in a while. I need to practice my ball handling. I'm trying out for the basketball team."

"I'm going to be a cheerleader," Toya stated. "While you're working with her, I'll practice my cheers."

"If your dad says it's okay, I'll take you," he responded. He often spent Sunday afternoons with his nieces.

They were soon in his SUV en route to the park.

Kyle parked near the basketball court. He was glad there wasn't a game going on. He could work with his niece without people running all around them.

He and Joi claimed one end, while Toya took the other, practicing her cheers.

Kyle had Joi perform ball slaps as the first drill.

"Remember to use your fingertips," he told her. "Palming the ball makes it more difficult to control it."

Kyle checked on Toya, then turned his attention back to Joi. "You're doing great, sweetie. Okay…dribble the ball hard—the harder you dribble, the quicker it's back in your hand. Keep your head up at all times, Joi."

He noticed a woman and a little girl nearby. The woman's hair was a familiar mass of tousled curls.

Phillipa. Kyle recalled how his hands used to get lost in those tresses. Her daughter resembled Phillipa even down to the laughter—she was a mini version of her mother. Her thick, curly hair was tamed in a ponytail that bounced playfully as they walked.

"Isn't that the lady you work with?" Joi asked, basketball in hand.

"Yes. That's Phillipa Stevenson with her daughter."

"She's very pretty and really nice, Uncle K. I liked

talking to her. Grandma's right. You should try to get her back."

He placed an arm around Joi. "I need you to focus on your ball handling—not my love life."

She laughed. "Are you gonna go over there and talk to her?"

"I think she wants to spend quality time with her daughter. Just like I'm over here doing the same thing with you and Toya. I'll see her tomorrow at work."

Joi wasn't giving up. "We can at least say hello, Uncle K. Besides Toya and I want to meet her daughter."

Her sister ran over to where they stood on the basketball court. "Uncle, isn't that your friend? The one who came to the house with you."

"I'm trying to get him to go over and talk to her," Joi stated.

"It's the polite thing to do," Toya interjected. "You know that's what Grandma would say."

He was outnumbered. There was no point in trying to win this battle.

"Okay…" Kyle said. "We'll say hello and then we're coming back over here." He hoped Phillipa wouldn't be upset with him for disturbing her afternoon with her daughter.

Phillipa blinked twice. She was surprised to see Kyle at the park and coming toward her with his nieces in tow.

"Mama, isn't that the guy you work with?" Raya asked.

"Yes."

"He has twins?"

"No, they're his nieces."

"Before you lay into me, I want you to know that it

wasn't my idea to come over here," Kyle began. "The girls wanted to say hello."

"It's not a problem," she said with a smile. She greeted Kyle's nieces and introduced them to Raya. Once the girls were talking happily, she murmured to Kyle, "Do you always throw your nieces under the bus like that?"

He chuckled. "Naw. I just didn't want you thinking I was stalking you."

"Give me some credit. I know you better than that," Phillipa said.

"You're telling me that you were okay with seeing me at Mert's?"

"I was surprised to see you there. I thought you weren't a fan of the place."

"I wasn't when we were together," Kyle responded. "I guess you can say it grew on me over time."

The twins and Raya wanted to go back to the basketball court, so Kyle and Phillipa watched them get back safely. They stood at the edge of the court and talked.

"Would it be too much to ask you and Raya to have lunch with us?" Kyle inquired.

"As long as we're going Dutch," she responded.

"You can at least let me pay for your meal, Phillipa." She eyed him stubbornly.

Kyle sighed in resignation. "Okay, fine."

"The twins are really sweet," Phillipa said. "Looks like they are growing into great young ladies."

He nodded. "Yeah, they are. Toya is more like her mother. Quiet and reserved. Joi… She takes after my mom."

Phillipa chuckled. "Oh, wow… Another Amelie."

"They named her Joi Amelie, and it fits her."

"I'm sure they miss their mother a lot."

"They do," Kyle responded. "They were so young when she died, but Jon tells them stories and he's captured a lot of memories of her on video."

She eyed him. "You're very good with them."

"Thanks. You know I've always loved children."

He had. Phillipa decided to change the subject to the case, as long as he was here. It was a safer topic anyway. "I keep wondering why Helena was brought here," she said. "Why the gazebo? The killer could've discarded her body anywhere." She glanced over at Kyle. "Do you think it means anything?"

"I don't know," he responded.

"Leaving a victim's body in an unusual location is a conscious criminal action. It can be done to impede an investigation, shock the finder, or give some sort of perverted pleasure to the killer," Phillipa stated.

"So, you think the gazebo means something? Do you think it's a message?"

"I don't know, but we have to consider all avenues." Phillipa looked over her shoulder to see if the girls were close enough to hear their conversation.

"They're still at the basketball court," Kyle said.

They walked in that direction.

"I came here on Wednesday after work," she stated. "I was sitting in the gazebo when I felt this strange sensation come over me. I felt like someone was watching me."

"Why are you just telling me this now?" he asked.

"I considered that it might have been my imagination."

"Maybe not, Phillipa."

She shrugged. "It might have been some random incident."

"I don't think so."

"How would anyone know that we're investigating Helena's case?" Phillipa asked. "The two things can't be connected."

"If it happens again, I want to know."

"Sure."

"Mama, I'm hungry," Raya announced.

"Me, too," Joi said.

"I invited Phillipa and Raya to join us for lunch," Kyle announced. "She said yes."

The girls cheered.

"Since she's saying yes, you might want to ask her out or something," Joi said.

Phillipa's mouth dropped open. "Does she know…?"

He nodded. "You can thank my mother."

They burst into laughter. At least the girls' presence was keeping things more lighthearted than awkward, despite there being plenty of potential for awkwardness where Kyle and Phillipa were concerned.

They decided to eat at Newton's, a place that came highly recommended by the twins.

"A booth okay?" Kyle asked.

Phillipa nodded.

A server came over to take their drink orders shortly after they were seated.

Phillipa and Raya shared a menu.

"You have to try the shrimp tacos if you like seafood," Joi said. "If you're wanting a burger, then this is the right place. They have the best cheeseburgers. You can even have mushrooms, bacon or avocado on them.

I always get mine with mushrooms. Uncle K likes avocado and bacon on his."

"Thank you for those recommendations," Phillipa responded. "Sounds like you can't go wrong with either choice." She glanced over at Kyle and grinned.

"I guess you know what I'm getting," he said.

Phillipa nodded. "I think I'll try the shrimp tacos."

"You won't be disappointed." Kyle gave the collar of his shirt a gentle tug, straightening it.

She eyed his movements and wondered if he was nervous.

"Mama, I'm going to have a cheeseburger," Raya announced.

"And the strawberry lemonade?" Toya said.

Her daughter grinned. "That's what I always order if they have it on the menu."

"Raya loves any flavor of lemonade," Phillipa said. "There's this one place we used to frequent in Los Angeles. They served lavender lemonade. It was delicious."

"Isn't lavender a flower?" Joi asked.

"Yes," she replied. "Some lavender is edible. They used dried lavender."

"It's purple," Raya interjected. "That's my favorite color."

"Oooh," Toya said. "Do you know how to make it?"

"I do," Phillipa answered. "The ingredients are water, sugar, honey, lemon juice, and dried lavender. Some people add food coloring to make it a vibrant purple."

"We're gonna have to make it," Joi said. "I bet Daddy would love some."

"What about me?" Kyle asked his niece. "I might want to sample this purple lemonade myself."

Joi chuckled. "We'll give you some, too."

The server returned to take their orders.

While they waited for their food to come, the twins and Raya talked about their schools and the different sports they played.

"They're getting along well," Kyle said.

Phillipa nodded in agreement. "Looks like it."

"I always knew you'd be a wonderful mother."

Her eyebrows rose in surprise. "Why do you say that? I'd never held a baby until Raya was born. I wasn't sure I even liked kids back then. But when she was born, it was love at first sight."

"I thought so because of the way you responded to them whenever we had to go into a home. You always kept stuffed animals in the squad car. I also noticed how you'd kneel down whenever you talked to them. It was like coming down to their level."

She nodded. "I didn't want to traumatize them further. It was easier for me. When I had Raya, I called my mother at least every other day with questions."

"You should've seen me the first time I held the twins. I think I almost gave Helena a heart attack."

Phillipa chuckled. "Oh, goodness…"

"Uncle K almost dropped me," Toya interjected. "Daddy told us that he was so nervous because we were really tiny babies. He said Uncle K wouldn't touch us after that."

She saw the look of embarrassment on Kyle's face and broke into laughter.

"Really?" he said. "You're gonna laugh at me like that?"

"Yes," Phillipa responded.

The server came with a huge tray laden with burgers and tacos.

Kyle blessed the food before they dived in.

Phillipa sampled her shrimp taco. "Joi, you're right. This is delicious."

"You should try one of the burgers next time," she replied before biting into her cheeseburger. "And add mushrooms. Super good."

"My birthday is next weekend," Raya announced. "We're going to eat pizza and go to the movies. After that we're going back to my grandparent's house for birthday cake, ice cream and a sleepover. Would y'all like to come?"

"Yeah," the twins said in unison. "Our dad's birthday is on Sunday. We just have to be back for the cookout."

Raya looked at her mother. "Is it okay, Mama?"

"Sure, it's fine. The more the merrier."

"I only invited two girls from my school," Raya said. "I don't have that many friends here in Charlotte."

"Well, now you have two more," Joi responded. "Toya and I are cool. We don't have drama."

Phillipa glanced up at Kyle and smiled. "I love these girls," she murmured.

Spending this time with the twins only reinforced her determination to find out the truth about their mother.

"I like Mr. Kyle," Raya blurted when they were on the way home.

Phillipa glanced over at her daughter in surprise. "Really?" She wasn't sure how Raya was going to respond to Kyle, especially once she learned of their past relationship.

She nodded. "He's really nice."

"Yes, he is."

"Mama, why didn't you marry him?"

Phillipa had to stop herself from slamming on the brakes. "H-how did you know about that?"

"I heard you and Grandma talking about it."

She chewed on her bottom lip as she tried to come up with a suitable response. "It was a long time ago, Raya. You know you shouldn't go around listening to grown-up conversations."

"I know." After a moment, she said, "I really like the twins, too. Thanks for letting them come to the party."

"It's my pleasure. Joi and Toya seem really sweet."

Raya nodded. "I think we're gonna be good friends."

Phillipa smiled. She hoped for the same.

"Toya said something about her mom dying when she was little," Raya said softly. "Did you know about that?"

"Yes, baby."

"I don't ever want to lose you, Mama. I don't think I'd ever get over it."

She reached over and took her daughter's hand in her own. Phillipa gave it a gentle squeeze. "That's why it's important for us to enjoy every day the good Lord gives us." Despite feeling sometimes like the Lord wasn't hearing her prayers, she was grateful to Him for every day she had with her daughter.

"You sound like Grandma."

She laughed. "She'd love to hear you say that."

Phillipa was glad Raya didn't stay focused on her and Kyle. She didn't want to discuss her relationship woes with her daughter.

A part of her wished she could fully erase her feelings for Kyle. Although she still felt a deep connection to him, one that seemed to grow as she'd enjoyed lunch with him and his nieces, Phillipa wasn't sure she'd ever be able to trust him again.

But more than that, she couldn't help but wonder if she was allowing pride to get in the way.

As soon as they arrived home, Raya rushed inside to tell her grandmother about Joi and Toya.

"I'm so happy to hear that you're making new friends," Bethany said.

Raya sniffed the air. "Grandma, did you make chocolate chip cookies?"

"I did. Why don't you go upstairs and get your bath out of the way. I'll have a plate of cookies and milk waiting for you when you're done."

"Yessss!" Raya yelled as she ran up the stairs.

"You've just made her day," Phillipa said.

"Does she know about their mother?" Bethany asked.

"One of the girls mentioned that she died when they were little. Raya has no idea that she was murdered or that I'm investigating her death. I'd like to keep it that way. Kyle said he'd talk to the girls."

"You saw Kyle, too?"

"He was at the park with the twins."

"Then you all had lunch together."

Phillipa nodded. "We did, Mom."

Grinning, Bethany inquired, "Did you have a good time?"

She followed her mother into the kitchen. "Actually yes, but don't go reading more into it. We did it for the girls, so they could get to know one another."

"Is that what you're telling yourself?" Bethany inquired. "Here…have a cookie."

Phillipa took a bite and chewed slowly as she carefully considered her mother's question.

Kyle had thoroughly enjoyed spending time with Phillipa and Raya. It pleased him that the girls had gotten along so well.

After dropping Joi and Toya off, he drove home, where he spent the rest of the evening organizing the files in his office.

After a dinner of leftovers and a much-needed shower after the day at the park, he settled down in the living room to watch television, although his mind was elsewhere. As usual, Kyle couldn't get Phillipa out of his thoughts. He was attracted to her even more, despite his efforts to resist all emotion where she was concerned.

It was a great to spend some time Phillipa outside of work and in a more relaxed environment. Tomorrow they would be back at work soon enough.

He appreciated the effort she'd put into Helena's case so far. Kyle prayed that Jon would not be devastated even more by what Phillipa had found out about Helena's past. His brother had already suffered more than any man should have to.

Kyle recalled the point where Phillipa was laughing at him. The memory made him smile. He knew it was all in good fun, and he'd always loved the sound of her laughter. It started off low, then rose as it overtook her. She'd always put a hand over her mouth whenever she couldn't seem to control it.

He hadn't realized just how much he had missed hearing her laugh until today. Kyle hoped they would have more moments like those in the future.

He stayed downstairs until it was almost midnight then retreated to his bedroom.

Kyle didn't go to bed right away. He sat up reading for a while.

He finally decided to put the book away when his eyelids grew heavy. His eyes landed on a photograph of his parents.

"I want a marriage like yours," he whispered.

His father was gone, and his mother was finally starting to see someone socially. She and Pastor Brady were going on an official date in a few days.

Kyle was happy for her. It wasn't his wish or Jon's for their mother to be alone. She deserved more.

He felt the same way about Phillipa. Only he hoped that she'd eventually come to realize that he could be the man in her life who would make her smile and fill her with laughter.

Chapter Twelve

"Clara was born in June," Phillipa announced on Monday. She'd walked over to Kyle's desk to inform him of her latest discovery. "Not March like we initially believed. This is a copy of her real birth certificate."

She handed the document to Kyle.

"I'm beginning to think that everything about Helena was a lie," he said. "Her name, birthday… Who knows what else."

He sounded a bit irritated. Phillipa knew it was because he was thinking of his brother and how he would be affected by these new revelations. "I'm convinced that she was running away from something. We just have to find out what it was and if her past caught up with her."

"What are you planning to do now?" he asked.

"I'm not really sure. We don't have any solid leads—and that really frustrates me."

"Phillipa, you've gotten further than any other investigator with this case," Kyle stated. "You're really good at this job, so don't give up. If anybody has a chance at solving this case, it's you."

She smiled at him. "I appreciate you saying that. I'm not ready to give up. I just feel like I'm missing an important piece somewhere."

Phillipa walked across the tile flooring to her desk, which was cluttered with folders, notes and photos. She picked up a picture of Helena and drew a ragged breath. "I'm doing the best I can," she whispered. "To be honest, I'm feeling a bit helpless at the moment. But don't worry. I'm going to find your killer."

Phillipa sat down, mentally reviewing everything she'd learned so far. As usual, she was left with nothing but more questions.

She peered at Kyle who was on the telephone talking. Phillipa wanted his insight, but he was working on another cold case with some strong leads. That file was his priority at the moment.

A shiver ran through Phillipa as thoughts about Kyle flooded her head. He was the man she'd always envisioned as her happily ever after. He hadn't changed much over the years; he'd matured. That much she could tell. If only he hadn't thrown their future away.

The following Saturday, Phillipa treated Raya and several of her friends to pizza and a movie.

"I can't believe you turned down buttered popcorn and you had a salad instead of pizza," Raya said as they exited the theater. "You love that stuff."

"I do, but I haven't been to the gym since we arrived, sweetie," Phillipa responded with a chuckle. "I got on the scale this morning and I've put on five pounds."

Raya shrugged. "Mama, you look great."

Joi and the rest of the girls nodded in agreement.

"You girls are so sweet," Phillipa said with a smile. "I'm saving my calories for birthday cake."

They headed to her SUV.

Phillipa unlocked the doors. "Sergeant Stevenson, I thought that was you," came a voice from behind them. Phillipa turned to see Paula standing there. "What a precious little girl. Is that your daughter?"

"Miss Johnson," Phillipa said.

"I saw my girls with you." She held out her arms for the twins.

Joi and Toya jumped out of the car and rushed to Paula.

Phillipa ushered Raya inside the vehicle, then watched as the twins hugged her.

"What are you girls doing here?" Paula asked.

"We went to the movies," Joi responded. "It's Raya's birthday. Daddy's birthday is tomorrow."

"Yes, I know."

"Now we're going to her house for a sleepover," Toya announced. "See you later."

"Yeah, see you later," Joi said.

When they were back in the SUV, Phillipa headed to the driver side.

"How are things coming along with Helena's case?" Paula asked, following her.

"Fine," she responded. She didn't want to discuss her work on open cases with anyone outside the department, and especially while she had a vehicle filled with young girls. "If you will excuse us, we need to get going."

"Oh, but I—"

Phillipa cut her off by saying, "Feel free to call me during office hours." However, she didn't have any intention of telling Paula anything.

* * *

Sunday after church, Kyle headed to Jon's to help his mother prepare for the cookout. They were celebrating his brother's birthday.

Amelie retrieved a covered pan laden with raw fish from the refrigerator and set it down on the counter. "I sure hope Paula don't come over here trying to take over. I'm not in the mood for her today. I had a wonderful time at church, and I don't want her to ruin it."

"I don't know why Jon invited her in the first place," Kyle responded. "Sometimes I wonder if he likes the attention."

"I think it's because of Helena."

Frowning, he asked, "What do you mean?"

"Helena loved Paula. Maybe he thinks this is what she'd want him to do," Amelie said.

"You're probably right," he responded, then picked up a can of beans. "I'll make the baked beans."

Amelie seemed caught up in her preparation of the rest of the food, seasoning the meat for the grill. "Thanks, sweetie."

He placed a large pot on the stove.

"Have you decided if you're staying in the Cold Case Unit?" she asked.

"How did you know I was thinking about leaving?"

"I figured now that Phillipa is back, you'd want to transfer out."

Kyle grinned. "We get along, Mom. There's no need for me to leave."

Amelie cut her eyes at him. "You know what I mean, son. I know you're taking that sergeants' exam. I know you'd rather be in Robbery."

"Is there anything you don't know?" he asked with a chuckle as he poured the beans into the pot.

"I invited Phillipa and her family over for the cookout," his mother announced. "Maybe you can try and work things out."

"I don't think it'll happen." Kyle had considered inviting Phillipa himself but wasn't sure how she'd feel about it. He decided to leave it up to Jon or his mother. He knew one of them would reach out to her, and sure enough, Amelie had extended the invite when Phillipa dropped the girls off that morning. She'd declined, saying that they were taking Raya to her favorite restaurant for dinner.

His mother glanced over her shoulder at him. "Now, I know you're not about to give up on something you want. This is not my child talking like that."

Kyle chuckled. "We're in a good space right now. I'm not going to mess it up. We both want to focus on Helena's case. That's the priority right now."

"I understand." Amelie began making hamburger patties. "Just don't give up. I know Phillipa still cares for you."

Kyle added barbecue sauce, a family recipe, to the beans. "If so, she's not ready to give me another chance, Mom. I'm going to give her the space she needs."

Amelie nodded. "It can't hurt."

Two hours later, Kyle was outside on the patio firing up the grill. The twins were outside sitting by the pool, while Kyle's mother moved about the kitchen applying the finishing touches to the meat.

When she was done, Jon carried it outside to the grill. "Here you go."

Kyle saw his niece sitting by herself. He walked over to the lounge chair. "What's up, Joi?"

"Nothing," she responded.

"Where's Toya?"

"She went up to her room to play video games."

"What's wrong?" Kyle asked, noting the unhappy look on her face.

"I wish God had let my mommy stay with us. Daddy would be so happy if she were here to celebrate his birthday."

"We all hate when someone has to leave us behind," he said. "I wish my dad and your mom were still with us. I miss them both, but then I remember that they're in Heaven. That's not a bad place to be, don't you think?"

"I guess not. It's never a bad thing when you get a chance to hang out with the Father."

He smiled. "Your mother will always be with Jon and with you and your sister. She lives in your heart."

"In my heart, she can never die," Joi said.

"Exactly."

"Uncle K, I hope you and Miss Philli will find the person who killed my mom."

"We're doing everything we can to do so. I promise you."

"We didn't say anything around Raya."

"I appreciate that."

"Does she know what her mom does?" Joi asked.

"I'm not sure to what extent," Kyle responded.

She seemed to take that in. "Can I help you with the grill?"

"Why don't you go help your dad? I bet he'd really love to show you how to make his famous potato salad."

Lowering his voice, he said, "I'll tell you a secret. Your mom taught him how to make it. It's her recipe."

Her eyes widened in surprise. "Really?"

Kyle nodded and placed a finger to his lips.

"I won't say anything." She ran into the house, with a lighter spring to her step.

Kyle chuckled to himself. "Jon's gonna kill me..."

It was true that Helena had first taught his brother how to make potato salad; however, over the years, Jon had experimented and improved the recipe. He kept his ingredients to himself, promising only to share it with his daughters. Not even Amelie knew what all went into his potato salad. Well, at least she pretended not to know whenever Jon was present. He had a feeling she'd figured it out a while ago.

He would have loved being able to give his brother the one gift he wanted—the identity of Helena's murderer.

Paula arrived a short time later wearing a pair of tight jeans and a cropped top. She walked up to Kyle and said, "I have a case of soda in my car. Could you get it out for me?"

"I'm on grill duty," he responded.

"I'll stay here until you get back."

"How did you get them in the car?" Amelie asked from behind her.

Paula pasted on a smile, then turned to face his mother. "Hi, Mrs. Rossi."

"Kyle's busy cooking the meat," his mother said. "If you need help, c'mon, I'll give you a hand."

"You're right. I was able to get them to the car. I'll bring them inside."

He heard his mother saying, "I told you we didn't

need anything else. We appreciate all you do, Paula, but you know we don't drink a lot of soda around here."

"I was thinking about your guests…"

"C'mon," Amelie said. "Ain't no point in bringing in the whole case. We won't need but a few."

Kyle shook his head. One day Paula was going to listen to his mother, or they would never get along.

Jon walked outside. "I thought I heard Paula."

"You did. She and Mom walked to her car. She brought soda."

Jon chuckled. "I know Mom didn't like that."

He nodded with a chuckle.

"Is Philli coming?"

"I'm not sure," Kyle said. "Mom invited her, but they have plans. I think they're still celebrating Raya's birthday."

Jon smiled. "The girls had a great time at the sleepover. It's all they've been talking about."

Kyle checked on the meat.

"Nobody could grill like your father," a familiar voice said.

He glanced over his shoulder, then turned to face Phillipa. "I didn't think you were coming today… I would've invited you myself, but I didn't want to make it awkward for you."

"I thought as much," she responded with a smile. "Raya decided she'd rather come here than eat at her favorite restaurant. She wanted to hang out with the twins. My wallet isn't complaining."

He was thrilled that she'd had a change of plans. "Your parents come, too?"

"Yes, they're in the kitchen with your mom," Phillipa said. "And Paula."

"Where's Raya?" he asked.

"She's upstairs with the girls."

Kyle told her about his conversation with Joi.

"I really didn't know what to tell her."

"Sounds to me like you said the right thing," she stated. "There aren't any easy answers in a situation like that."

"You two really look good together," Paula said, suddenly appearing by them. "It's a shame it didn't work out between y'all."

Kyle glared at her. "Do you need something?"

"Your mom wants to know if the hamburger patties are ready."

"In five," he responded.

"Sergeant Stevenson, I'd like to speak with you at some point," Paula said.

"I'll be here," Phillipa responded. "I'm not going anywhere. However, I hope it's not the same conversation we had yesterday."

"No, it's not," Paula responded before walking away.

"What happened yesterday?" Kyle inquired.

"We ran into her after we left the movie theater. I had a car full of girls and she's starts asking me about Helena's case. I told her to reach out to me during office hours."

"I know she was Helena's friend, but why is she so interested in the case?" he wondered aloud. "Outside of being nosy."

"I have no idea," Phillipa uttered. "But I intend to find out."

A smile tugged at Kyle's lips. If Paula had any sense, she wouldn't try to make an enemy of Phillipa.

* * *

Phillipa's patience with Paula was almost to its limit. She couldn't understand how Jon had put up with her for so long. She touched Kyle's arm and said, "I'm going to check in with your mom. See if she needs help with anything."

"*We* have everything covered," Paula interjected. "Just hang out here and enjoy yourself. It's a party after all."

"Why is she acting like the lady of the house?" she asked when they were alone.

"Because she thinks she will be one day."

"That much is clear," Phillipa said.

"It's never going to happen."

"How can you be so sure?" she asked. "Jon may really care for her. I don't see how he could put up with Paula all these years if he didn't. Face it…she might end up being your sister-in-law."

"I don't see it happening," Kyle responded.

She chuckled. "You really don't like her."

"I don't. And I don't think Jon does either."

Phillipa decided to let the subject of Paula drop when Jon walked outside.

"Happy birthday," she said.

He hugged her. "Thank you. I'm glad you came."

She smiled at him. "I wouldn't have missed it."

The food was ready shortly, and everyone gathered to fix their plates and eat.

Phillipa caught Paula watching her several times. At one point, she considered confronting the woman, but decided it wasn't worth it. She didn't want to do anything to mar Jon's birthday celebration.

"I think she's jealous of you for some reason," Kyle whispered in her ear as he sat down beside Phillipa.

"I don't know about all that, but she's interested in me for some reason." She wiped her mouth on a paper napkin. "Maybe you've been wrong about Paula. I'm beginning to think it's *you* she wants."

Kyle almost choked on his lemonade.

"You okay?" She handed him a napkin, then burst into laughter. "You should see your face right now."

"I can't believe you just said that."

Phillipa shrugged. "It makes sense to me."

Kyle picked up his burger. "I can tell that you're enjoying this."

"I am," Phillipa admitted. "Great job on the grilling, by the way. Your dad would be proud."

She wasn't aware she was staring at him until he caught her.

Phillipa looked away. "Have you seen Raya?"

"She's with the girls over by the pool," he responded.

She glanced over her shoulder. Her daughter looked like she was having a great time with Joi and Toya. They were sitting in lounge chairs eating and talking. She smiled at the sound of Raya's laughter.

"She's happy."

"How about her mother?" Kyle asked. "Is she happy, too?"

"I am," Phillipa said. "Coming home was the right decision."

"I'm glad to hear you say that. I didn't want you to regret coming back."

"I could never regret it. I missed my parents terribly when I was in California, but I loved my job. When this opportunity came along to head the CCU, it was perfect timing."

Their conversation came to a sudden halt with the appearance of Jon and Paula, who joined them at the picnic table.

"We're not interrupting, are we?" Paula asked.

"No, not at all," Phillipa responded. She picked up her cup of lemonade and took a sip.

Paula sliced into her hot dog with a plastic knife.

"I've never seen anyone do that," Kyle said. "Why don't you just pick it up and take a bite?"

Paula sent a sharp glare in his direction before pasting on a smile. "There's more than one way to eat a hot dog."

Shrugging, he responded, "Yeah, I guess you're right."

"Sergeant Stevenson...or do you mind if I call you Phillipa?" Paula asked.

She nodded. "Phillipa is fine."

"What made you decide to leave Los Angeles and come back to Charlotte?"

"This is my home," Phillipa responded. "It just made perfect sense."

"I'm certainly glad you came back," Jon stated.

"So am I," Kyle interjected. "You've been great for the CCU."

She smiled. "It's nice to be appreciated."

Paula eyed her but didn't say a word.

"Hey, are you still crazy about Cook-Out?" Jon questioned.

"I am," Phillipa said with a short chuckle. "The only thing is I can't eat them as much as I used to because I don't want to add pounds."

Paula wiped her mouth on the edge of her napkin. "I'm so glad I don't have to worry about my weight. If anything, I need to gain."

"You're lucky," Phillipa said in response.

"To be honest, I wouldn't mind another five or ten pounds," Paula responded. "What do you think, Jon?"

He grinned. "You could use a few extra pounds."

Phillipa furrowed her brows in surprise at his comment. "See, that's why I don't ask questions like that."

Paula laughed. "He's always been brutally honest."

She nodded in agreement. "This is true."

Jon chuckled. "If you really don't want to know the truth, then don't ask me or Kyle."

They all laughed.

For the moment, Phillipa found herself enjoying Paula's company. She was a bit self-absorbed but was pleasant enough to be around.

After the cake was served, Phillipa prepared to leave. She walked over to Kyle and said, "It's time we head home. Raya needs to get ready for school."

"I'm glad y'all were able to join us."

She smiled at him. "Me, too."

Phillipa sought Jon out next. "We're leaving but thank you for including us."

"It felt like old times with you here."

She didn't say it, but Phillipa felt the same way. His parents had hosted several barbeques during the summer and would always invite her. They had always made her feel as if she were a part of the family.

She said her goodbyes to Amelie and the twins, gathered her daughter and her parents and left the house.

On the way home, Raya said, "I had so much fun.

The twins are really cool. I like that they don't treat me like a little kid."

"I don't want you to grow up too fast," Phillipa responded as she glanced up in the rearview mirror. Her daughter sat behind her in the back seat beside her grandfather.

"Mama, it's gonna happen. Just don't treat me like a baby in front of people."

"I won't."

"You know your mother is still my baby," Bethany said from the front passenger seat. "No matter how old you get, you will always be your mother's little girl."

Raya chuckled. "I know…"

As soon as they walked into the house, Phillipa sent her daughter upstairs. "Go on and get your bath out of the way."

"Your mother and I are going to watch a movie," her father announced. "Do you want to join us?"

"I'll watch TV with Raya for a little while," Phillipa responded. "I need to get my clothes ready for work this week and make sure that daughter of mine does the same."

She went upstairs a short while later.

Raya had just come out of the bathroom and was in the process of selecting what she was going to wear to school.

"I'm about to toss in a load of laundry," Phillipa announced. "You have anything that needs washing?"

"I did my laundry Friday after school since it was my birthday weekend," Raya said.

Phillipa eyed her in amazement. "Oh wow…look at you…great job, sweetie."

She went to her room to retrieve the basket of clothing that needed washing, then carried it to the laundry room located upstairs.

Ten minutes later, she joined Raya in the loft area to watch television.

"What are we watching?" she asked.

"I'll let you pick," Raya responded.

Phillipa cherished moments like this. Her daughter was a year older; Raya was growing up so fast. She thought of Helena and how she was no longer around to watch her daughters come of age. Phillipa realized just how lucky she was to have such a presence in Raya's life.

Kyle thought of how much Helena had missed of her children's lives as a wave of sadness washed over him. He was grateful that they seemed happy and secure, but he knew there were times when they yearned for their mother.

Today had been a good day, he decided. Jon celebrated his birthday surrounded by family and close friends, including Phillipa, much to Kyle's delight. Even Paula had not gotten on his nerves as she normally did. Maybe it was because Phillipa held most of his attention the whole afternoon.

There had been no tension between them—a good sign that they were no longer tiptoeing around one another outside of work. Memories from their past welled up and flooded his mind. He was glad Phillipa had come home even though they weren't exactly on speaking terms in the beginning.

Kyle cautioned himself not to get his hopes up. She was his supervisor. He didn't want to tread in what could become dangerous waters. He had to wonder if he could stay in the CCU despite his growing feelings for Phillipa. Kyle closed his eyes while considering the question, then opened them when he got his answer.

He'd heard talk that there would be an opening in Robbery coming up—had even mentioned it to his mother. He'd stuck around CCU to make sure the case didn't remain on a shelf in storage. Now that Helena's case was in Phillipa's hands, he was okay with leaving CCU, but he would try to stay long enough to see Helena's killer brought to justice.

Chapter Thirteen

Phillipa swallowed her irritation as she walked out to the lobby area to meet her visitor. "Miss Johnson, I didn't expect to see you here."

"Can we talk in your office?" Paula asked.

She looked uncomfortable, so Phillipa said, "Sure, but I only have a few minutes. What can I do for you, Miss Johnson?"

"Just call me Paula," she said as she walked into Phillipa's office. She sat down in one of the visitor chairs. "I was in the area, so I thought I'd stop by, since we didn't finish our conversation from the other day. I wanted to speak with you at the cookout, but you left before I had the chance."

"All right. Paula, what's your interest in this case?" Phillipa asked. "I thought I'd made it clear to you that I'd only update Jon."

Paula sighed. "Helena wasn't just my friend. She was more like a sister to me. I feel like I have a right to know what's going on with her case."

"I see."

"You sound as if you don't believe me."

"I only look at the facts, Paula," Phillipa responded.

Her almond-shaped eyes narrowed. "What exactly do you mean by that?"

Phillipa met her gaze straight on. "I'm not convinced that you and Helena were as close as you try to make it sound."

Paula's lips turned downward. "Excuse me?"

"In my experience, a friend tends to protect the reputation of the victim. You were only too willing to cast a bad light on Helena during our initial interview. I'd like to know why?"

"I was simply telling the truth," she huffed, clearly offended by Phillipa's words.

"Have you shared this *truth* with Jon?"

"No, not really," Paula responded. "But only because I didn't want to hurt him or the girls." She chewed on her bottom lip a moment before asking, "Isn't there anything you can tell me?"

"All I can say is that we're still investigating Helena's murder."

"Do you have any suspects?"

"There's nothing else I can tell you."

"Regardless of what you may think about my friendship with Helena—I loved her, and I want to know who killed her."

Phillipa nodded. "If that's all, Paula, I need to get back to work."

Paula stood. "Thanks for nothing."

"You have a nice day, too."

As she watched the woman leave her office, Phillipa hoped that was the last she'd see of Paula Johnson.

Kyle was surprised to see Paula walking out of Phillipa's office when he returned from having lunch with

Jon. He looked over to Bryant and asked, "When did she get here?"

His friend shrugged nonchalantly. "I don't know. I just got back about ten minutes ago. You'll be happy to hear that I was shopping for an engagement ring."

Paula walked up to him before Kyle could say anything. "Maybe I'll be able to get some answers from you," she said with an angry huff.

"About what?"

"Helena's case. What else?" Bryant's brows rose as he stepped away and sat at his own desk.

"We're investigating it," he responded. Out of the corner of his eyes, he glimpsed Phillipa watching them. "There's nothing I can tell you."

"Your brother must be so frustrated with you right now. He's been waiting for twelve years to get answers."

"Jon will be the *first* to know anything about Helena's case, Paula. You don't have to worry about my brother."

"But I *do* worry about him, Kyle. I care deeply for Jon. I know that bothers you, but there's nothing you can do about it."

Kyle shook his head. "I need to get back to work."

"I won't keep you any longer," Paula stated. "But I will say this... I'm sure Jon's not going to be happy with the way you and your ex-fiancée are treating me."

"I'll take my chances with my brother," Kyle responded.

She glared at him before practically stomping out of the precinct.

"That woman is something else," Phillipa said, walking up to his desk.

Kyle shook his head. "She probably thinks Jon will marry her once the case is closed."

He added, "Jon is just being nice to her. If she weren't the girls' godmother, he would've told Paula to get lost a long time ago."

Phillipa laughed. "I'm still not quite convinced that Paula's not after you."

"Don't start that up again."

She laughed even harder. "Actually, I could see you married to her. You'd have a cute little house with a white picket fence and two point five children."

"I'm not the white picket fence type," Kyle responded. "Remember?"

When they were engaged, he and Phillipa had had a huge argument over the choice of fencing for the house they'd wanted to buy.

"I do," she said. "I remember the fight we had. Looking back, it was so silly."

"The color of the fence was really important to you."

She smiled. "I just thought white looked so much prettier than the unfinished fence you wanted."

"That was so we could decide what color we wanted after the house was built."

She laughed. "It makes sense to me now," Phillipa said. "Back then, I just wanted to have my way. I'm not so sure I was as ready to get married as I thought."

Kyle was surprised to hear her say this.

"I think I was as scared as you were," she stated quietly. "I was just too proud to admit it."

Phillipa looked at the clock, then back at him. She cleared her throat. "Do you want to help me create a timeline of the last two weeks of Helena's life?"

"Sure. I have to meet with a witness on another case, but I'll be back in about an hour and a half."

"That works," she responded. "Good luck with the witness. Is it the Gowen case?"

"Yes."

"It's been five years—hopefully, the wife will remember something more."

"I'm beginning to think we might need to move her to our suspect list," Kyle said. "Some things just don't add up." He gave her a brief update on what he'd found to support his theory.

"Keep me updated," Phillipa said.

He smiled. "Will do." Kyle felt he was close to bringing his case to closure. He hoped they would soon be able to say the same about Helena's case.

"I don't know about you but I'm starving," Kyle said two hours after he returned from interviewing his witness. "I'm sure you could hear my stomach protesting all the way over there."

Phillipa chuckled. "I couldn't hear it over mine, I'm afraid."

"Why don't we get out of here and grab something to eat? There's a great restaurant a couple blocks away."

Phillipa shook her head. "I don't think so." The tension that once filled the air had completely dissipated, but she wasn't sure going to dinner with Kyle was a good idea.

"Why not?" he asked. "We work together, Phillipa. It's not a date or anything."

She paused. Phillipa decided she was overreacting. "I guess it can't hurt," she responded finally.

"Do you want to ride with me?" he asked.

"I'll drive," Phillipa said. "I can head home straight from the restaurant after we eat."

Kyle walked over to his cruiser while she got into her SUV.

Phillipa followed him to the restaurant. She parked beside him, then got out.

Candles, fresh flowers in vases and plants littered every tabletop in the restaurant they walked into.

"Do you know what you're getting?" Phillipa asked after they were seated and took a few minutes to scan the menus.

"I think I'm going with the chicken club sandwich," Kyle responded. "What about you?"

"There are too many choices."

"Yeah…some things really haven't changed," he uttered with a chuckle.

Phillipa gave him a sidelong glance. "What are you talking about?"

"You always had a hard time deciding on what to order."

"Like I said…too many choices. I've never been here before, so I don't know which entrée will taste best."

"I know how much you love pasta," Kyle said. "Try the Cajun chicken Alfredo. They serve it with roasted tomatoes. It's delicious. You can also get it with shrimp."

"Hmmm…it does sound good." Phillipa looked over at him. "Why are you just ordering a sandwich? I thought you said you were hungry."

"It's what I have a craving for. Plus, I love their sweet potato fries, which come on the side."

Phillipa warmed under his gaze. "You do realize that you're staring at me," she said as she laid down her menu.

"I'm sorry," Kyle responded. "I didn't mean to stare, but I couldn't help myself. You're still a very beautiful woman, Phillipa."

She waved her hand in dismissal. "Things are really good between us right now, so let's not go there."

He shrugged good-naturedly. "Hey, I was just giving you a compliment. I didn't mean any harm."

"None taken, but it's not necessary," she stated.

He laughed.

And she flushed. "You're right," she said after a moment. "I'm overreacting."

The moment of tension passed when the server came to take their orders, and thankfully, his humor kept Phillipa on the verge of laughter while they waited for their food. Soon she found her eyes straying to his face, his caring eyes, and staying there.

"Now you're the one staring," Kyle said.

"I got a little caught up in memories."

He shifted his position in the seat. "It's been that way for me a long time."

"I wasn't sure we'd be able to ever sit down like this and share a meal again."

"I know," he responded. "You're going to find the person responsible for Helena… Clara's death, right?"

"I'm going to do my best."

His phone started to vibrate and he checked it. "I need to take this."

She busied herself checking her own phone while he took the call.

"That was the alarm company," Kyle announced after hanging up. "For some reason, my alarm went off at the house." He rose to his feet. "I don't think it's anything, but I still need to check it out."

"I'll go with you," Phillipa said.

"It's not far from here. Do you want to ride with me?"

"No, I'll follow you there. I'm not sure how long this may take."

They found their server on the way out of the restaurant, and Kyle explained they had to leave but asked to get the meals packed up when they were ready. They'd come back to pick up the food. He handed her three twenties. "Keep the change."

As soon as they arrived at the house, Phillipa's gut instinct was to go for her weapon as she got out of her SUV.

When Kyle got out of his cruiser, she noticed he also had his hand on the handle of his Glock 22. He walked around the perimeter, looking for any tracks that might belong to an intruder.

She slowly made her way to the wooded area at the back of the house. Phillipa's calm was interrupted by the sound of crackling leaves. She whipped around, prepared for battle.

"It's just me," Kyle said. "Everything out here looks normal. Let's check inside the house."

As she followed him into the house through the back door, Phillipa recalled that she and Kyle had once dreamed of living in a place like this—hence the discussions about a fence. She couldn't help but wonder what might have been if they had gone through with the wedding.

He entered his office, looking around.

"Someone was in here," he said. "My papers have been moved around."

"Is anything missing?" she asked.

"Not that I can tell."

After checking every room downstairs, Phillipa followed him up a flight of solid wood stairs. "Are you sure you don't have some woman after you?"

"That is the only thing I'm absolutely sure of," Kyle responded. "I haven't seriously dated anyone in almost a year."

"Maybe it's a fatal attraction."

He gave a short chuckle. "Not hardly."

Right away Phillipa noticed the spacious bedrooms on the second floor. The owner's suite was expansive, with large bay windows. She tried not to pay much attention to Kyle's home.

She turned and left the room.

Kyle joined her. "Nothing looks out of place up here."

"You really think someone came into the house?" Phillipa asked.

"Yeah," he responded. "But they didn't take anything."

"I'm surprised you don't have any cameras installed."

"That's changing first thing tomorrow."

"You should have CSI come check for fingerprints."

"Whoever it was, they parked in the driveway and came in through the front door. Almost as if they had a key."

"Does anyone in your family have a key to your place?" Phillipa asked.

"Just my mom. It wasn't her because she has the alarm code. She would've turned it off as soon as she walked in."

"They must have known you didn't have any cameras. Which suggests that you might know your uninvited guest."

"Or they just decided to take a chance," he responded. "I don't know what they could've been looking for..."

"Do you think it has anything to do with Helena's case?" Phillipa asked. "Or one of the other cases you've been working on? Maybe the Gowen case now that the wife is on your suspect list."

"That's what I'm thinking, but the question is which one."

Kyle's eyes traveled the room once more before he turned to Phillipa. "I'm going to wait here for CSI. Do you mind picking up our dinner?"

"Not at all. I'll be back shortly."

A few minutes later, Phillipa was in her SUV and on her way back to the restaurant.

It didn't take long for her to pick up the food and head back to Kyle's house.

Crime scene technicians were there when Phillipa returned.

"How long have they been here?" she asked.

"About five minutes," Kyle responded. "You can go on and eat."

"I'll wait for you. I just need to call my mom and check in with Raya."

He nodded in understanding.

After her phone call, Phillipa walked over to Kyle saying, "I can't believe someone actually broke into your house. This is really crazy."

"I agree. And I'm inclined to believe it's connected to the Gowen case, but I can't say for sure."

"Why the Gowen case and not Helena's?"

"Mattie Gowen and her brother are both at the top of my list. He's been arrested in the past for burglary, and he's been avoiding me for the past two weeks."

After the technicians and the police officer left, Kyle warmed up their food. "We finally get to eat dinner," he said.

Phillipa placed a hand to her stomach. "Good because I'm so hungry."

"Me too."

They sat down at the table.

Kyle quickly blessed the food.

"I still wonder if the intruder is someone you know well," Phillipa said.

"But why break in?" he wondered. "And why chance triggering the alarm?"

"Maybe they thought they knew your code," Phillipa offered.

"I change it every three months. The only people who know this are my brother and my mom."

They finished their meals, each lost in thought.

Phillipa pushed away from the table. "I hope you enjoyed your sandwich as much as I enjoyed my pasta."

Kyle smiled. "I did. I was so hungry, I had to keep myself from swallowing it whole."

She laughed.

Their gazes met and held.

The last thing Phillipa wanted was to give Kyle the impression that this dinner was a step toward something more.

She cleared her throat softly, then said, "I should get home. I don't want Raya to worry. I'll help you clean up first…" Phillipa wanted to put some distance between them emotionally and physically. She needed a moment to refocus and get her feelings in check.

Kyle shook his head. "You don't have to do that. C'mon, I'll walk you to your car."

"You have a really nice house," she said as he led her to the door.

"Thanks," he responded.

Kyle did as he said and made sure she made it safely to the SUV.

"I'll see you tomorrow," she said before climbing inside.

Phillipa waved before pulling onto the street and driving away.

As she drove, she pondered the break-in further. Nothing was missing, so there weren't any clues. Maybe the alarm scared the intruder off before they could get whatever they were after.

But why risk going into a house and setting off the alarm? Whoever it was had to be desperate, Phillipa decided.

Kyle remained on his porch long after watching Phillipa drive away until he couldn't see the lights of her SUV anymore. He appreciated her show of concern when he'd gotten the news of the alarm going off. He knew it was genuine and it touched him.

There was a moment after they'd finished eating that Kyle was tempted to get out of the chair, throw caution to the wind and kiss Phillipa, but he'd restrained himself. While kissing her would've been worth it, it also would've been a mistake. He had to be content with their relationship as it was. Kyle didn't want any more tension between them.

Kyle looked up and down his street, searching for an unfamiliar vehicle parked nearby. He was fairly sure that whoever had broken into his house was long gone. It gnawed at him that he didn't have a clue as to the identity of the intruder. He was going to have cameras installed as soon as possible. The invasion of his home angered him.

He went inside and locked his door.

Kyle returned to his office and sat down at his desk. As he went through the files on his desk one by one, he realized that there *were* at least three missing. Among them was Helena's file.

He quickly surmised that the intruder was most likely only interested in one of the cold cases but had taken the other two to try and throw him off.

Kyle considered calling Phillipa, then changed his mind. She was probably with Raya, and he didn't want to interrupt their time together. What he had to tell her could wait until tomorrow.

He spent the rest of the evening thinking about the three cases and trying to figure what information the intruder was after.

None of it made much sense to him. Maybe after a good night's sleep he'd be able to take a fresh look and come up with some answers.

Chapter Fourteen

"You and Kyle seem to have found some common ground," Bethany remarked as she finished cleaning the kitchen the next morning after breakfast. She placed the damp dish towel on the oven handle.

"Things are better between us," Phillipa responded as she leaned against the counter with her arms folded. "Kyle and I agreed to put aside our differences while we're at the precinct."

"And outside of it?"

She smiled. "We're working on a friendship, I guess."

"It's a shame your dinner was interrupted last night though. I'm glad you two are spending time together outside of work."

"Mom, that was just dinner between two people working on a case. We worked late and got hungry."

Bethany looked at Phillipa. "I think it's time you knew the truth."

She gave her mother a sidelong glance. "What truth?"

"Kyle came to us a few months after you left. He told us that he was going to California to work things out with you. He said he was going to marry you and would even stay out there with you if that's what you wanted."

Phillipa dismissed Bethany's words with a slight wave of hand. "That was just talk, Mom."

"No, he was serious."

"I never heard from him," Phillipa said.

"That's because you'd told us that you were marrying Gary," Bethany responded. "Your father told Kyle you were engaged."

"Why didn't you or Dad tell me about this sooner?"

"Would it have changed anything?"

"Maybe… I don't know," Phillipa replied. "I honestly don't know, but I should've had the choice."

"Honey, you'd already accepted Gary's proposal. I don't believe you would've backed out of that— especially after what you went through with Kyle."

Phillipa knew her mother was right. She would've gone through with her marriage to Gary. Because that's exactly what she'd done. The day before they got married, Phillipa had an anxiety attack. No one knew—not even her parents. She wanted her marriage to work, but even then Phillipa had doubts that it would survive.

"You should've told me, Mom. I went all those months thinking he really didn't care…"

Bethany's eyes teared up. "If we were wrong, then I want to apologize to you. At the time, I thought I was doing the right thing for everybody. Hon, I'm so sorry."

"I know you thought you were looking out for me," Phillipa said, hugging her mother. "I love you for it, but this is something only I can work out. Me and Kyle."

"You're right, sweetie. Your father and I never should've interfered."

"The truth is that I should have listened to you, Mom.

You tried to tell me that Gary and I should wait instead of rushing down the aisle. You knew I wasn't ready."

"I knew you were heartbroken over Kyle. I felt you needed a little more time to heal."

"I was too stubborn to admit that you were right," she admitted.

"And yet if you'd listened to me, we wouldn't have our beautiful Raya," Bethany said. "She's the blessing that came out of your marriage."

Phillipa smiled. "You're right about that. I'd do it all over again to have that little girl in my life. Besides, Gary was really a sweetheart." A tear slid down her face as she gazed at Bethany in earnest. "But, Mom, I never should've married him. He deserved someone who loved him. I hurt him…" She wiped her face with her left hand. "I broke his heart."

"Oh, honey…" Bethany tried to comfort her, but the guilt of what she'd done to Gary was like a heavy weight—one she carried around with her every moment of every day.

The next day, Kyle didn't know what to expect when Phillipa summoned him to her office.

"What I want to discuss with you is personal," she stated. "If you're not busy for lunch, I'd like to meet with you then."

"No plans other than eating."

She smiled. "Around noon?"

"I normally don't go until one o'clock, but that's fine."

"One o'clock works for me," Phillipa responded.

He didn't dare hope that she was ready to finally have the all-important conversation with him. Kyle still had deep feelings for Phillipa and had respected the boundaries in place. She was slowly letting her guard down around him, so he didn't want to do anything to put the progress he'd already made with her at risk.

She was at his desk at one o'clock sharp, and they drove to Dillon Park.

Phillipa led him over to a hot dog stand. "I was surprised to see that Mr. Tony was still in business."

"He has stands all over the city now," Kyle said.

"Do they still taste the same?"

He nodded. "Yeah."

After getting their food, they walked over to the gazebo.

"I'm glad it's empty," Phillipa said. "I wanted us to have some privacy."

"This sounds serious," Kyle responded. "Am I in some sort of trouble?" He was trying to make light of the situation. He needed to tell her about the missing files, but he'd wait and listen to her first.

She smiled. "No, you're not in trouble."

Phillipa sat down on the bench. "My mother told me that you were planning to come to California until you found out about Gary."

So she knew about his plan to win her back. "It's true," he responded before biting into his hot dog.

"I didn't know anything about this until this morning."

"I'm not sure it would've changed anything," Kyle said with a slight shrug. "If I thought it would, I would've taken the first flight out to Los Angeles."

She looked down at her own hot dog. "I don't know how I would've responded. I just wish my parents had told me." After a moment of hesitation, Phillipa said, "I wish you'd come to California."

Did she? "Your parents wanted to tell you, but I asked them not to say anything to you. I'd already made a mess of things. I didn't want to do it a second time. You were happy."

"I thought I was," Phillipa murmured softly.

"Huh?"

"Nothing," she said. "It seems like a lifetime ago."

"Not to me," Kyle responded. "It feels like yesterday."

"Would you have really stayed in Los Angeles?" Phillipa asked.

"Yeah."

She smiled. "It's nice to know."

Phillipa finished off her hot dog.

"If I'd come, would you have talked to me?" he asked.

"I think so. Your coming after me would've reassured me that you still cared about us. About our relationship."

"The only reason I didn't fly out there is because I thought you had truly moved on with Gary. I loved you, but it was more important to me that you were happy—even if it meant I would be miserable for the rest of my life."

They sat in silence for a few minutes.

"There's nothing we can do about it now, but I appreciate you telling me this," Phillipa said quietly.

He wanted to put his arms around her, to pull her close and kiss her. Instead, Kyle pushed the thought away and they walked back to the car.

"Do you have any updates on Helena's case?" Kyle asked. He thought it best to return to business. He sensed from Phillipa's mood that changing the subject was the best course of action in the moment.

"I've learned that Myra Rowland's family lives in Columbia, South Carolina. They left Miami a year after her death. I'm thinking of driving there to speak with the victim's mother. Maybe she can help sort out the Clara/Helena mystery."

"Do you want me to go with you?"

"I can handle it."

"I don't think you should go alone. You don't know anything about these people or how they're going to respond to your questions. I promise to sit back and let you take the lead. I won't say anything, but I'll have your back."

"Since you put it that way... sure. Come with me as long as you can spare the time with your other case-work?" she stated.

"Not a problem," Kyle responded. "You're the boss."

Phillipa looked at him and asked, "Does that bother you?"

It didn't bother Kyle at all. After all, he was the one who'd recommended her for the position. Although Phillipa didn't have any knowledge of this.

"No, not at all." He paused a moment before saying, "Oh, I went back through my office, and I discovered that there are three files missing."

Phillipa stopped short. "Really?"

"Yeah. One of the files missing is Helena's case."

"Who are the other two?" Phillipa asked.

"Roger Dunn and Christina Danforth. I suspect the intruder is only interested in one of those files."

Phillipa nodded in agreement. "But which one?"

"That's what we have to find out."

* * *

Phillipa replayed her earlier conversation with Kyle over in her mind. She wasn't sure what would've transpired if he had come to see her in California. She felt deep down that if Kyle had shown up, she never would've married Gary.

The night before her wedding, she'd had a dream that he appeared at the chapel to whisk her away with him. During the ceremony, Phillipa anticipated his showing up and interrupting the service.

But he never came.

She was forced to go through with her vows. Forced to marry a man she didn't love. All because she believed that the only way for Kyle to prove his undying love for her was to chase after her.

Phillipa wanted to kick herself for being so juvenile during that period of her life. She had reacted to Kyle not coming to California by hurting Gary, an innocent in all this.

But she hoped that Gary knew that there was a part of her that cared for him. Phillipa had just never loved him. She accepted her role in the breakup of their marriage and felt badly. She didn't realize just how guilty she'd been feeling about what she'd done until now.

"You remember the times we used to come to Columbia?" Kyle asked the next morning when they were on their way to meet with Myra Rowland's family.

Smiling, Phillipa nodded. "I loved shopping at the Soda City Market. I used to have so much fun there. I'd always be exhausted by the time we left, but it was great seeing so many vendors. I went home broke after each trip, but it was so worth it."

He nodded in agreement. "They still hold it every Saturday from nine to one."

"Rain or shine," she interjected with a chuckle.

"Back then, you wanted to drive down every Saturday after that. Man, you'd get so angry when I didn't want to go."

"I did, but then your shift changed, and you had to work… I didn't want to come alone, so I talked my mom into it a couple of times." Phillipa glanced over at him. "Have you been back?"

"The twins and I have been there a few times," Kyle responded. "But every time I came, it just reminded me of you."

Phillipa stared out of the passenger side window. "You're just saying that."

"No, I mean it."

She turned to look at him. "You say that, but you never once tried to reach out to me after I left."

"I figured you didn't want to hear from me," he responded. "Especially after you got married. You know that messed me up."

"No, I didn't know," she said. "I didn't think you cared one way or the other."

"What did you expect me to do? Kidnap you before your wedding?"

"Well, it would've been something."

"I can see it now," Kyle said. "I show up and you shoot me in the kneecap."

Phillipa burst into laughter. "You remember that?"

"Yeah. You told me if I came to the house, you'd shoot me in the knees."

"What did you really expect? You'd called off our wedding."

"I believed you."

"I meant it," Phillipa responded.

They looked at one another and laughed.

"I wouldn't have shot you," she said a few minutes later.

"You say that now. I know that temper of yours, Phillipa."

"That was a long time ago. I've evolved since then."

This was the first time Phillipa had been able to laugh about the past. Maybe she was evolving.

"Here we are," Kyle said an hour later. "Agnes Rowland's home. I hope she has answers for us."

"So do I," Phillipa responded.

They walked up the concrete steps to the porch and rang the bell. A full-figured woman with ginger-colored locs, who looked to be in her thirties, opened the door.

"Hello, I'm Sergeant Phillipa Stevenson and this is Detective Kyle Rossi. We're here to see Agnes Rowland."

"What do you want with my mother?" the woman asked, her hands on her generous hips.

"I'm working on a case, and Myra Rowland's name has come up."

"Myra was my sister. My mom is in a nursing facility. She has advanced dementia—she won't be able to help you."

"What is your name?"

"Regina. I'm Regina Rowland." She invited them in and led them to the living room, then gestured for them to sit. "My sister's been gone a long time, so I don't know why her name would come up now." Regina sat down across from them on a floral love seat. "What is this about?"

"Did you ever hear the name Helena Douglas?" Phillipa asked.

"No, I never heard that name mentioned before."

"But you did know Clara Davis?"

Regina nodded. "Oh, yeah. I knew her. Clara, Myra and this other girl, Kelsey, were very close. We used to call them the Three Musketeers. Things changed when Clara started seeing that drug dealer Savage. Then I noticed he and Myra started spending time together. He was giving her money and clothes... I kept telling my sister that he was nothin' but trouble." Regina shook her head. "I knew things were gonna go wrong when she started messing around with Savage behind Clara's back."

"Did Clara ever find out?"

"I don't know for sure. I was away at school. I went to college in Jacksonville." She shrugged. "It's possible she did because I heard that they got into a fight. When I asked Myra if it was over Savage, she denied it. She told me that Savage had broken up with Clara. She told me Clara was cool with her seeing him because she was involved with someone else by then."

"How did you find out that Myra was seeing Savage?" Phillipa asked.

"I was home on break. I grabbed her cell phone by mistake, and I saw text messages between the two of them. I confronted her. I told her she was being foul. She told me that Savage was in love with her—not Clara."

"What can you tell me about the night your sister disappeared?" Phillipa asked.

"She left the house to meet up with Clara," Regina said. "That's all I know. You should probably talk to my brother, Miller. He was the last person to see Myra."

"How can I reach him?"

"He's in pharmaceutical sales and travels a lot. He's out of town now. I'll give you one of his business cards." She stepped out of the living room and disappeared down the hall.

When Regina returned, she said, "I don't know what any of this has to do with your case, but I believe all the way to my gut that Savage killed my sister and Clara. He played them both, and when he got tired, he murdered them. He probably killed this Helena person, too. What goes around comes around though… Somebody shot and killed him."

"Thank you for your time," Phillipa said, taking the card. "I appreciate your talking to us. One more thing, what was Savage's given name?"

"Leroy Brown."

Phillipa looked over at Kyle, then asked, "Is he related to Kelsey?"

"I think they were cousins. She really didn't have anything to do with him though. Kelsey was the smart one of the three. She didn't run around at parties and clubs like Myra and Clara. Don't get me wrong—they were tight, but Kelsey was different. She acted older."

"Thank you again."

Phillipa swallowed her irritation. They hadn't gotten a lot of new information. They were already aware of the girls' friendship and that Savage was a suspect before he was also murdered.

They would have to try and put the pieces of the puzzle together with what they knew, which wasn't much.

Chapter Fifteen

"Do you think that Clara was running from Savage?" Phillipa asked when they were on their way back to Charlotte.

"That would be my guess. He had Myra killed. Clara knew it and left Miami, changed her identity and started a new life."

"Then why stay in hiding after Savage died?"

"Okay," Kyle said. "He had an alibi, so this means that he most likely had someone else kill Myra. Whoever that person is, he was still a threat to Clara."

"I can buy that," she responded. "But do you think she faked her death all on her own? Because I don't. I think she had help with that and with establishing her new identity."

"My guess would be her father," Kyle responded. "He and his brother owned a funeral home, so they would certainly have the means to fake a death…"

Phillipa glanced over at him. "I think you're onto something."

"Savage died within months of Myra's death, so while he may be responsible for that one, we know for sure that he didn't kill Helena," Kyle said. "I never thought this case would become so complicated. I don't know how Jon's going to react when he finds out his life with Helena was based on a lie."

Phillipa looked at him. "Don't say anything just yet. I want to have this whole thing sorted out first."

"Oh, I won't," Kyle responded. "Besides, I wouldn't even know where to begin."

She settled back in her seat. "Kelsey and Savage are cousins…"

"It's a dead end."

"We have plenty of those," Phillipa said. "One more won't matter. I'm just wondering why she didn't mention it when I talked to her, but then Kelsey never brought up Savage during that conversation."

"She probably didn't think it was important."

"Hmmm," she murmured. "Even though he was a suspect?" Phillipa paused a moment, then said, "Let's talk about something else. I need a mental break from the case."

"Fine by me. What do you want to talk about?"

She glanced over at Kyle. "Why didn't you ever marry?" She'd been wondering since reconnecting with him. "You must have met someone who made you consider settling down at some point."

"Not really," he responded.

"Nobody?"

"I came close once, but I didn't want to settle. It would've have been unfair to her."

Phillipa understood because that's what she'd done to Gary. "You did the right thing."

"I learned from the first mistake I made," he said. "With us."

"Do you really feel that way?" she wanted to know.

Kyle nodded. "Not about postponing the wedding, but letting you leave town and then not coming after you…that was my mistake."

Phillipa felt it was easy for Kyle to talk this way because there was no way they could act on their feelings now. Too much time had passed. And she was his supervisor.

"You're quiet… What's on your mind?" he inquired.

"I'm your boss. The most either one of us could ever hope for is friendship."

Kyle contemplated her words in silence. Phillipa was right, of course. CMPD frowned upon romantic relationships between supervisors and subordinates, but it wasn't exactly law. However, policy dictated that a romance between a supervisor and subordinate would result in the mandatory transfer of one of the involved parties. They would also have to notify the captain of the courtship.

He'd already decided to apply for an opening with the Robbery Division. Kyle was also studying for an upcoming promotional assessment.

Phillipa would find out eventually about his immediate goals, but Kyle decided to keep quiet for now. He didn't want her to get the impression that he was being presumptuous regarding a relationship.

They were back in Charlotte and heading to the precinct.

"What do you think about grabbing something to eat before we dive into work?" He wasn't ready to share her with the rest of the team.

"Sure," Phillipa responded. "Cook-Out?"

He laughed. "Works for me."

"I'm getting the honey mustard chicken wrap."

"What did you do? Memorize the menu?" Kyle asked with a chuckle.

She glanced over at him. "And if I did…"

"No need to be defensive."

"I'm not."

The expression on her face sparked more laughter in him. "I'm sorry, but I can't with that petulant look on your face."

Phillipa laughed. "You make me sound like a spoiled little girl determined to have her way."

"Your words."

Some of the good humor left her face. "Do you really think of me like that?"

"In all the years I've known you, Phillipa—you want things your way and it's often not negotiable."

After a moment of tense silence, she said, "Okay that stung, but I can't deny the truth."

They turned into the parking lot and pulled into the drive-thru lane.

"What I said wasn't meant to be a negative, Phillipa."

She gave him a tiny smile. "I know. Regardless of how you meant it, you were right. I've always preferred to have things done my way. I was selfish."

"In some areas, but not most," Kyle responded. "You are the most caring person I know. You're always trying to help others and you're generous. I still remember how you'd buy up gowns when they were on sale and donate them to girls who couldn't afford dresses for prom. I bet you still volunteer at homeless shelters when you can."

"I still do those things, but when it comes to the men

in my life—that's when I'm truly selfish," Phillipa said. "Love is about selflessness."

They placed their order.

"Phillipa, I'm not going to let you do this," he said. "Nobody is perfect. I was even selfish at times. We were good together."

"Yes, we were," she responded.

"Then let's just leave it at that," Kyle stated. He hadn't meant to get so personal with her. He didn't want to make her uncomfortable. Changing the subject, he asked, "So do you think you're really going to hear from Myra's brother?"

"I'm not sure." Phillipa said. "But then I didn't really expect to hear from Kelsey."

After paying and retrieving their food, she parked so they could eat.

"I never expected this case to become so complicated," Kyle said. "I always figured it was just a random murder. That some bloodthirsty killer laid eyes on Helena and shot her."

Phillipa bit into her chicken wrap.

After wiping her mouth on a paper napkin, she said, "It's definitely not a random killing. Someone targeted your sister-in-law. They wanted her dead."

Later that day, Phillipa sat in her office compiling all her notes on Helena.

"So…Myra was seeing Savage behind Clara's back," Phillipa said aloud. "Myra told her sister that Clara was okay with it. She was fine with being replaced by one of her friends…" Phillipa shook her head. "I'm not buying that."

She got up and walked over to the whiteboard in

her office, where she'd pinned photos of Myra, Helena and Kelsey.

Then she stood there staring at them.

"Kelsey's pretty much a nonentity," she whispered. "So is Savage."

Phillipa picked up another photo of Clara during her college days and pinned it next to the other one of her. She wrote *Clara/Helena* underneath them.

She paced as she tried to mentally piece together all she'd learned, and she often found it helpful to talk it out aloud.

Why would two friends who were as close as sisters end up dating the same man?

It didn't make sense to her, but it wasn't exactly a unique situation with Helena. An image of Paula formed in her mind.

You didn't do such a good job when it came to picking your friends, Helena.

Phillipa wondered if Helena had known of Paula's attraction to Jon. She walked over to her desk, picked up the receiver and dialed Amelie's number.

"Hey, Miss Amelie." The other woman greeted her, and after some small talk Phillipa asked, "I have a quick question. Did Helena ever give you the impression that Paula was interested in Jon?"

"No, she had some blind trust in that woman. Plus, Paula wasn't as blatant with it back when Helena was alive. She acted more like a friend."

"That's what I needed to know. Thanks, Miss Amelie."

"You're welcome."

She hung up and returned to the whiteboard. Phillipa had uncovered Helena's secret, but they still had no suspects. She felt like she hadn't gotten anywhere with this investigation, and it frustrated her.

Kyle came to the office shortly after six o'clock. "You need any help?"

"What I need is a new perspective," Phillipa responded as she sat down at her desk. "Myra and Clara seeing the same man..." Her voice trailed off.

"What is it?" he asked. "I can almost see your mind working. What are you thinking about?"

"What if Myra and Clara had a fight over Savage? What if she accidently killed her friend?"

"That doesn't sound like the woman I knew," Kyle said.

"But it would give her a reason to run and change her identity."

"True," he responded, "but Helena couldn't hurt anybody. You're reaching with that one, Phillipa."

She sighed in resignation. "You're probably right. I don't even believe it myself."

"Why don't I order some food," Kyle suggested, "and we can talk this through."

Phillipa nodded. "Okay."

Thirty minutes later, they were eating Chinese food while going back over the details of Helena's murder. Again.

Two more hours passed, and they still hadn't gotten anywhere. But in that time, she had been tensely aware of Kyle's presence. It was as if something had shifted between them after their conversation earlier.

Kyle sat in a chair with his back to her now. He was staring at the whiteboard.

Phillipa wasn't expecting a breakthrough with the case tonight, but she could sure use one. "Why don't we call it a night?" she suggested as she rose to her feet. "We're just going around in circles."

"You're right," Kyle admitted. "We've been over this case so many times and all we've come up with is more questions."

Phillipa left her desk to stand once more in front of the whiteboard. She eyed the information there.

Kyle got up from his seat and joined her.

Her eyes met his gaze and lingered there. Phillipa wasn't sure when the atmosphere in the room changed, but it had.

Almost as if they had no control of their actions, Kyle leaned forward, kissing her. She didn't try to stop him because Phillipa wanted his kiss.

Realizing that they were still at work, she broke it off. "I guess we got a little carried away just then," Phillipa said.

"I have a confession. I've wanted to do that from the very first moment I saw you again."

"I guess we needed some closure, but it can't happen again, Kyle. We agreed to keep our relationship professional."

"Why is it so hard for you to forgive me, Phillipa?"

"Kyle, you meant everything to me. I loved you beyond reason, but you not only broke my heart—you broke me. My marriage and my faith in God paid the price for the hurt. Would it have been so easy to forgive me if I'd done the same to you?"

"No, I guess not," Kyle responded, shifting away. "I'd try to forgive, but it wouldn't be easy."

"I'm trying to work through everything."

"It's not easy seeing you all the time and remember-

ing how we used to be. But I'm trying to give you the
space you need."

"I know," Phillipa said with a smile. "I appreciate
your efforts, and they don't go unnoticed."

"I miss my friend."

"I don't have a problem being your friend, Kyle. I've
missed our friendship, too." She picked up her tote. "I
should get home to Raya."

"I'll walk you out," Kyle said.

As they headed toward the doors, Phillipa asked,
"Did you ever get cameras installed in your house?"

"Yes," he responded.

She got into her car, waved at Kyle, then drove out
of the parking lot.

He's really trying. There was a part of her that wanted
to trust him, to give Kyle another chance...

But Phillipa reminded herself that she couldn't think
about that right now. She had a case to solve.

The next day when she got to the office, Phillipa
found she had a message waiting from Miller Rowland.
She quickly returned his call.

"Thank you for calling me back," she said when he
answered the phone.

"My sister told me that you came by the house to
discuss Myra."

"Yes, I did."

"I might be able to help you with that. I'm actually
in Charlotte right now," Miller said. "If you'd like, I can
come by the police station in about an hour."

"That's perfect," she responded. "I'll see you then."

Phillipa got up and gestured for Kyle to come to her
office.

"I just got off the phone with Miller Rowland," she announced. "He's coming to the precinct in an hour."

"I'd like to sit in on the conversation," he said.

"That's fine." Phillipa respected Kyle's innate sense of discernment about people. He was a good judge of character. "I hope he can shed some more light on Clara and Myra's relationship."

"Me, too," he responded. "Hey, I hope I didn't make you uncomfortable last night. I shouldn't have brought it up—especially here."

"It's okay. I'm glad we talked. Really, I am."

He awarded her a smile.

"I'll let you know when Miller arrives," Phillipa said, needing to put some distance between them. Now that she was warming up to Kyle, long-buried emotions flowed like an erupting volcano.

Her eyes strayed to his lips at the memory of the kiss they'd shared the night before. She had definitely missed his kisses.

Phillipa abandoned the idea of that as quickly as it had come. He was her employee. As long as he worked in CCU, she would never cross that line.

Kyle felt a subtle shift in his relationship with Phillipa. He wasn't sure what it meant, but he was optimistic.

He and Phillipa both wanted to focus their attention on closing Helena's case. After that, Kyle had some decisions to make—one being whether to stay in the CCU. Regardless of what happened between them, he had to consider his career path.

Kyle went to the break room to get a cup of coffee. He

found Bryant in there reading a newspaper. He looked up and broke into a grin. "She said yes."

"Congratulations," he told him. "It's about time."

Kyle walked over to the table and sat down across from his friend.

"What are you gonna do?" Bryant asked.

"About what?"

"You've been alone a long time, Kyle. Aren't you lonely?"

"After my relationship with Janice ended, I promised God that until He brought Phillipa back to me, I wouldn't date anyone else. It wasn't fair to them because my heart belongs to another."

"Now she's back."

Kyle gave his friend a wry smile. "I know, but she's not ready."

"So, you're just gonna wait for her?"

"I am. Until Phillipa tells me that I shouldn't. I have to hear it from her."

Kyle wasn't listening to anybody else this time. He should have gone after her—all the way to the West Coast. Maybe he could've changed her mind about marrying Gary. It was just one of those things that he would never know what would've happened, and he needed to accept that.

This time, Kyle intended to follow his heart.

Chapter Sixteen

"Miller Rowland is here," Phillipa told Kyle. "I put him in Room One. Let me go in first. You follow shortly after."

"Okay," he responded.

Phillipa entered the room and introduced herself. When Kyle joined them a few seconds later, she handled that introduction as well.

She pasted on a smile, then said, "Thanks so much for coming in to talk to us."

She observed his blank expression, expensive suit, manicured fingernails and designer briefcase. "Like I said on the phone, I might be able to tell you more about what happened than Regina could," Miller said. "But first, I'd like to know why you're looking into Myra's case."

"We think your sister's case may be connected to a murder we're investigating," Phillipa said.

She had his full attention now. "Really? Who?"

"Helena Douglas Rossi."

He shrugged. "Never heard of her."

"If you don't mind, can you tell us about your sister?"

"Myra and I are twins," Miller stated. "We were very close. She confided in me often."

"Did you know about your sister and Savage?" Phillipa asked.

Miller nodded. "Yeah, I knew all about her relationship with that drug dealer. I kept telling her to leave him alone. I'd heard that he was also messing around with her friend Clara Davis." He paused a moment, then said, "I wish she'd listened to me."

"Regina mentioned that you were the last person to see Myra alive. What can you tell us about that day?"

He steepled his fingers. "My sister left the house that afternoon to meet up with Clara. She told me they were going to talk. They hadn't been speaking, but Myra wanted to change that. She told me that she wanted to patch things up with Clara. Myra told me that she realized Savage was no good. She said she was done with him. I'd heard that Clara had also kicked him to the curb. That was the last time I saw her alive."

"What do you think happened?" Kyle asked.

"I know what happened," Miller stated. "Savage killed my sister and Clara, too. I don't care about no trumped-up alibi. My family hasn't completely healed from losing Myra. Everybody loved her." He eyed Phillipa. "Why do you think her case is connected to this Rossi woman?" Miller asked.

"We're investigating all avenues," Phillipa responded.

"Okay, I get that…but how is your case connected to my sister's case?" Miller asked a second time.

She decided to be honest with him. "Clara Davis didn't die in 2006 as everyone believed," she said, her gaze never leaving his face.

Miller looked shocked. "What are you telling me right now? That she's still alive?"

"We believe that she didn't die until 2010."

Miller looked over at Kyle, then back at her. Shaking his head in denial, he said, "There must be some mistake. Clara died the same year as my sister…2006. I won't ever forget it. They found her body in Atlanta."

"We don't think the body that was found in Atlanta was Clara's. It was misidentified."

"I don't know what's going on here…"

"This is a photo of my sister-in-law, Helena," Kyle said. "Is this Clara Davis?"

"It looks like it could be her," Miller responded. "Just older. How did she die?"

Phillipa picked up the photo before saying, "She was shot."

"So if Clara changed her identity, she must have been scared about something," Miller surmised.

"Why do you say that?" Kyle asked.

Miller shrugged. "Sounds to me like she was on the run. I can't think of any other reason for her to change her name like that. She must have been in some kind of trouble."

"Why would Clara need to run?" Phillipa questioned.

"Maybe she witnessed Savage kidnapping and killing my sister. Maybe that's why she took off like that. I don't know. Isn't that your job to figure out?"

Phillipa didn't like or appreciate Miller's tone.

"When you find out what really happened, I hope you'll let me know," he went on.

She was curious why he'd become suddenly belligerent. He seemed more angry than grief-stricken.

"How often do you come to Charlotte?" Phillipa asked.

"I'm on my way to Virginia but stopped here just to talk to you."

"You don't service this area?"

"No. My territory is the DC, Maryland and Virginia region," Miller said. "I'm actually in the middle of buying a house up that way. If we're done, I need to get on the road."

"Thanks for coming in, Mr. Rowland."

"I hope you find what you're looking for," he responded.

Phillipa watched him until he left the building. She didn't care for Miller Rowland at all. There was a coldness to him. And a look that was almost sinister.

After Miller left, Kyle followed Phillipa into her office and took a seat. "What do you think of him?"

She sat down at her desk. "You mean about his theory of what happened, or the man himself?"

"What he said aligns with what we know," Kyle said. "As for the man himself—I didn't care for his attitude."

"I felt the same way. He seemed very angry."

Stroking his chin, Kyle said, "I got the feeling that Miller didn't like us investigating his sister's case."

"Then why bother coming in?" Phillipa asked.

"Out of curiosity?"

"Maybe…"

"He really didn't tell us anything we didn't already know," he said as he rose to his feet. "We're not giving up though."

She nodded in agreement. "I need to take a walk to clear my head. This is frustrating."

Phillipa headed out behind him.

Kyle sat down at his desk. He'd considered taking a walk with her, but assumed she needed some time alone. He understood how Phillipa felt; he was just as frustrated as she was, but he meant what he'd said— they weren't going to give up. Kyle couldn't explain it, but he felt they were getting close to finding the killer. He believed it.

Just like he believed that one day he and Phillipa would be together—he had faith. It was his faith that had carried him to this point. It was his faith that God would answer his family's prayer by revealing the perp responsible for Helena's death.

Kyle knew it would happen in a most unconventional way—the same way they'd discovered the truth about his sister-in-law. He hadn't taken time to process his feelings about Helena. He was disappointed in her for not being honest with the family. If she was in danger, she could've come to them for help.

Helena could've told Jon the truth and he wouldn't have abandoned her. He'd adored his wife and would have remained by her side until death. If only Helena had trusted him. Trusted them.

After a two-block walk, Phillipa returned to her office and closed the door. She sat at her desk, deep in thought.

Miller had seemed genuinely shocked by the news that Clara's death took place years later than he'd believed. It was obvious that he hadn't known the truth.

"Helena, why did you run away?" she asked aloud. *You were afraid. I'm sure of that. I just need to find out the reason.*

Her phone rang, interrupting her thoughts.

"This is Sergeant Stevenson," she stated when she answered it.

"This is Detective Bancroft with Miami PD. I'm returning your call regarding the Myra Rowland and Clara Davis cases."

"Thank you for calling me back."

"May I ask why you're interested in them?"

Phillipa decided to get straight to the point. "Detective, I believe Clara Davis didn't die in 2006 as everyone believed. She didn't die until 2010."

"There must be a mistake. Her body was found in Atlanta. Her own father identified the remains."

"It wasn't her body he identified, Detective Bancroft. Her father and his brother owned a funeral home. I believe they helped Clara fake her death. My theory is that she may have witnessed Myra's death. She left Miami and went to her father."

The detective then asked, "The case you're investigating...how did the victim die?"

"She was shot in the chest. Same as Myra," Phillipa responded. "She was also known as Helena Douglas Rossi. She was the wife of a heart surgeon and the mother of twins. We intend to have her remains tested for DNA, but we're looking to find out more about the victim."

She heard a sharp intake of breath, before he questioned, "Do you have a suspect?"

"No, I don't."

"A witness?"

"None," she replied.

"Friend of yours?"

"Her husband is a friend," Phillipa said. "He has no idea about any of this."

"I can send you a copy of the files on both Myra and Clara. Not sure what help they'll be though."

"Thanks," she murmured. "It doesn't hurt to take a look at them. Detective, did you speak with their other friend Kelsey Brown?"

"I did. She wasn't with them. She couldn't tell us much."

"Did she have an alibi for that day?" she asked.

"She was home with her mother."

After she hung up, Phillipa left her office and walked over to Kyle's desk.

"I just spoke with the detective in Miami. He's sending copies of Myra's and Clara's files."

"Did you learn anything new?" he inquired.

"Nope." Phillipa glanced up at the clock on the wall. "One thing though... I'd like to know more about Clara's father. He identified the body, claiming it was his daughter. It was either the act of a concerned father or one with something to hide."

"Why don't you take off?" Kyle suggested. "Spend some quality time with Raya. I'll see what I can find out about Helena's father."

"Thank you," she said. "I think I'll do just that."

Raya was working on a project when Phillipa arrived home.

"Hey, sweetie...need some help?"

"No, I can do it."

Phillipa navigated to the kitchen, where her mother was preparing dinner. "Can I help with anything?"

Bethany looked up and smiled. "You can make a pot of rice, if you don't mind."

"Not at all."

Phillipa retrieved a pot from one of the lower cabinets. "How was your day?"

"Good," her mother responded. "Amelie and I met for lunch and then we went shopping for rosebushes. She wants to plant some in Jon's backyard."

"I hope you two aren't doing any plotting to get Kyle and me back together."

Bethany chuckled. "Not at all, hon. We're staying out of that—you and Kyle will have to figure out how to get back what you had."

She poured two cups of water into the pot and turned on the heat. "Glad to hear it, Mom."

"Although I always believed that what you and Kyle had…it was worth fighting for," Bethany said.

"Is this you staying out of it?"

"I'm just speaking my thoughts. That is all."

Phillipa had once shared her mother's belief, but when Kyle didn't come after her, she decided she'd been wrong in her thinking.

She broke off that unsettling thought and focused on cooking a pot of rice as her mother requested.

"How's the investigation going?" Bethany inquired.

"It's taken several turns, but they all lead to dead ends," Phillipa responded.

"I'm sure you'll find the person responsible."

She smiled at her mother. "I bet if I told you I was going to fly to the moon, I'd have your full support."

"You sure would," Bethany responded with a chuckle. "I believe my daughter can do anything she puts her mind to doing."

Smiling Phillipa said, "I feel the same way about Raya."

She picked up the pot and took it over to the sink to drain the water off the rice.

"I tell her that all the time because I don't want her placing limits on her abilities."

"I remember when you told us that you wanted to be a police officer," Bethany said. "I was scared for you, but I couldn't let you know it. I just prayed for the good Lord to protect you throughout your career."

They continued their conversation while finishing up dinner. By the time everything was ready, her father arrived home.

While they ate, Phillipa observed the interaction between her parents with a heavy heart. A wave of envy washed over her. All she'd ever wanted was a loving husband and a family.

Raya was her joy, but Phillipa deeply desired the love of a man. The truth was that she wanted the love of only one man.

Kyle Rossi.

Her hand started to tremble so much that her fork fell from her fingers to her plate.

All eyes turned toward her.

Phillipa released a shaky chuckle. "I'm a little clumsy tonight. I guess I'm more exhausted than I thought."

After dinner, she spent some quality time with Raya before heading to her room.

Phillipa spent the rest of her evening thinking about the revelation she'd spent years trying to forget.

Chapter Seventeen

The next morning, Kyle met with Phillipa in her office.

"It's confirmed. Clara's badly decomposed body was identified by her father and taken to Davis Funeral Home for cremation. It was owned by Nelson and Elijah Davis. The funeral home is now run by Elijah's daughter. A Rosalie Davis-Cobb. She'd be Clara's cousin."

"We should talk to her."

"It's worth a shot."

"Let's call her now," Phillipa said.

He gave her the phone number, and she didn't waste a second before dialing.

"Davis Funeral Home… How may I help you?" a male voice answered.

"I'd like to speak with Rosalie Davis-Cobb," Phillipa said.

"Hold, please."

A minute later a new voice came on the line. "This is Rosalie Davis-Cobb."

Phillipa introduced herself, then said, "I'd like to ask you some questions about your cousin Clara Davis."

"You say you're calling from Charlotte? My cousin

died in 2006 and as far as I know, she's never been there. I think you may have the wrong person."

"I'd just like to verify a few things."

"Such as…?"

"What can you tell me about your cousin?"

"Not much. She and I weren't close. I hardly ever saw her."

"Did you see her when she came to Atlanta in 2006?" Phillipa asked.

"I didn't even know she was here. I don't think her dad knew either."

"Why do you say that?"

"I was working at the funeral home at the time. If Clara had come here, I would've known."

"Can you check to see if there was a Helena Douglas at the funeral home around that time?"

"Helena Douglas… No, I've never heard the name," Rosalie said. "I'm looking in our system. We never did a funeral for anyone by that name either. I'm afraid I don't understand what this is about."

"That's what we're trying to figure out," Phillipa responded. "I'll be in touch once we have all the information."

"Thank you… Clara and I weren't close, but I did care about her. If there is more information on who killed her, I'd like to know."

"We struck out again," Phillipa said after she got off the phone. "At some point we will need to test Helena's ashes."

Kyle shook his head. "I just don't know how or what to tell Jon."

"I wish I had some answers for you," she said. "I'm really sorry…"

"It's fine. I know you're doing your best. You must remember that we don't have the whole story yet."

"How can you be so optimistic?" she asked.

"I have no choice," Kyle said.

"Good. Because it's going to take divine intervention to help us close this case."

Phillipa was in a bad mood. She was frustrated with the way her investigation was going. She was disappointed in herself. She was also tired of being on an emotional roller coaster.

Phillipa's feelings for Kyle were confusing, and her resolve was weakening more and more. They worked in the same precinct—there was no escaping him.

She couldn't just run away. She was his supervisor. She couldn't avoid Kyle. She had to be more professional than that.

Phillipa spent the morning in her office with her door closed. She'd told her staff she was not to be disturbed.

Kyle sent her an email to let her know that he'd finally closed the Gowen case. The victim's wife and her brother were being booked downstairs.

Phillipa picked up the phone.

"Fantastic work on the Gowen case," she said when he answered. "I'd like to talk to you. Can you please come to my office?"

"Sure. Be there in a sec."

"Congratulations again, Kyle," Phillipa said when he joined her.

"Thank you," he responded, taking a seat. "We're on track to close the Marshall case, too. We have evidence that it was the cousin's gun."

"You're doing a wonderful job," Phillipa said, then paused when it seemed clear his mind was elsewhere. "What are you thinking about?"

"Us."

"What about us?"

"Do you miss us?" Kyle inquired. "The way we used to be? Because I do."

"We've been getting along well. Don't ruin it now."

"I'm not trying to ruin anything, Phillipa. I'm trying to get you to see that I still care deeply for you."

"Kyle, I hear you, but what exactly do you want me to do with that information?"

"Nothing. I mean… I don't like this wall between us."

She sighed. "I'm doing the best I can in this situation. I really am. If I'd known you were in CCU, I would've turned the job down."

"Why?"

"Because I didn't want this to happen. You ruined my marriage and now you're trying to ruin this job for me." Phillipa wanted to take the words back as soon as they'd left her mouth. "Kyle…"

"No," he interjected. "I get it. I'm sorry. No. You know what? I'm tired of apologizing. My timing sucked, but I still believe it was the right thing to do. I didn't want us to get married and then regret it. All I asked you for was a postponement. *You* ended the relationship."

He stormed out without waiting for a response.

Phillipa's eyes filled with tears. He was right. She was the one who had ended the relationship. She didn't give him a chance to fully explain what was going on with him because she was thinking only of herself and how it would look to everyone. She'd never really considered how Kyle was feeling or what this was doing to him.

Yet, he was going to come after her—Kyle had been planning to come to California. If only she hadn't been in such a rush to get married. She'd done it to prove that someone wanted her as a wife.

I've been a terrible person. I didn't deserve a man like Gary, and I don't deserve a man like Kyle.

Kyle wanted to be angry with Phillipa, but he couldn't stay that way. He knew the things she'd said were out of hurt. He understood what it felt like to be in pain. But he refused to drown in it. Although her words stung, Kyle didn't let them stick. He vowed to keep the faith.

Phillipa was his soul mate—the only woman in the world for him. Kyle believed this with his whole heart, so he would just wait until she was ready to accept his love.

In the meantime, he would help Phillipa with Helena's investigation—if she continued to allow him to do so. If she wanted him to step aside, he would do as she wished.

He went online to check the internal job openings. If he and Phillipa were to have a chance, Kyle would have to leave CCU. He was fine with that. He'd always considered CCU a temporary stop in his career, to find answers for his brother.

After reviewing the listings, Kyle returned his attention to the file on his desk. He pulled out the summary and began reading.

He forced himself to not seek out Phillipa's presence.

She wanted nothing to do with him at the moment, and he intended to respect that.

Kyle was thrilled when his mother called to invite him to lunch. Getting away from the precinct would do him good.

"I'll see you in thirty minutes," he said before hanging up.

Chapter Eighteen

Phillipa felt terrible about the way she'd talked to Kyle.
It bothered her to the point that she couldn't leave without having another conversation with him. She had to
make things right.

But it seemed he'd gone to lunch when she sought
him out.

"Can you let Kyle know that I'd like to see him?"
she asked Bryant.

"Will do."

When Kyle returned forty-five minutes later, he came
to her office. "Bryant said that you were looking for
me."

"Yes. Please come in."

He took a seat, his gaze averted.

"Kyle, I owe you an apology. I never should've said
those things to you."

He met her gaze. "Why not? You meant them."

"It was unfair to blame you. You've been great with
me."

"I've tried to be," he said.

"I'm sorry, Kyle. We have to work together, and I
don't mean to make it uncomfortable for you."

"I'm fine."

"No, you're not. I saw your face. I hurt you."

"I guess we've hurt each other," he responded, his tone resigned.

"Is it possible for us to start over?" she asked. "Like right now?"

"Phillipa...we don't have to do that. Look, all I want is for you to be happy. You're great for CCU and I'm glad you accepted the job. You have an amazing team— I hope you realize this."

"I do," she said. "We have a good work relationship and we're rebuilding a friendship, but there are times when that line between love and friendship gets blurred. For me anyway. I know it's because we have history, and it's not like we can forget that. What we had together was mostly good. I should've had faith in that, but I didn't. I'm as much to blame for what happened—if not more."

"I don't blame you for anything," he responded.

"This just proves that you're more mature than I am."

"I wouldn't say that."

She smiled. "You're proving my point."

He chuckled.

Phillipa held out her hand. "Friends?"

Shaking it, he said, "Friends."

When Kyle walked out of the office, Phillipa felt much better. She couldn't handle any more tension between them.

Kyle returned to his desk and sent up a prayer of thanks. "Thank you for softening Phillipa's heart toward me. Now, I just need You to work one more miracle. Give us Helena's killer and help us close that case."

The cloud of tension that usually wafted about whenever he and Phillipa were together was finally gone. He no longer felt like he had to walk around on eggshells. It was a great feeling. Kyle felt free to just be himself.

Nothing could spoil this day for him.

Kyle settled back in his chair, a smile on his face as he updated the arrest reports and related crime reports on the two cases he had recently closed. He proofed his follow-up reports, making sure that all the developments during his investigation supported his request to bring charges against the suspects.

He felt a pinch of sadness when he thought about his brother. But Kyle refused to let his faith waver.

He looked up and saw Phillipa pacing in her office. She was still trying to make sense of all they'd learned about Helena. He agreed with her that there was a huge piece of the puzzle still missing.

We just need that piece.

Kyle prayed they would find something soon. Jon had been patient with them so far, leaving them to work the case and not asking too many questions, but soon he would want some answers. And neither he nor Phillipa wanted to tell him only part of the story. They didn't want to leave him with nothing but speculation either.

Sitting there, Kyle's mind was fraught with different scenarios. He twirled his pen as he tried to figure out something. None of it was making sense, however.

From the expression on Phillipa's face, he figured she was probably doing the same thing.

We're not quitting! Kyle wanted to shout to her. They were not going to give up on Helena. He didn't care that she'd lived a lie—Helena still deserved justice.

* * *

"Good morning," Phillipa greeted him when Kyle walked into the conference room. They had a unit meeting scheduled. Kyle was the first to arrive.

"My mom's birthday is coming up," he said. "Jon and I are throwing her a party. Would you please come? Your parents are also invited. Jon has someone to watch the girls, so if you like, you can bring Raya over—she can have a playdate with Joi and Toya."

"It's not Paula, is it?" she asked, trying to keep her expression neutral.

"No. It's Jon's next-door neighbor."

"I'd love to come," Phillipa said. "You know how much I love your mother."

"Did you know that she and your mom have been hanging out together?"

"I know they meet for lunch every now and then."

Kyle laughed. "Once a week. I don't have a problem with it—I just think it's interesting."

"Do you think they're up to something?" she asked.

"I don't know. But I wouldn't be surprised if they were. My mom would love to see us together."

"So would my mother," Phillipa said.

They looked at one another.

"Yeah, I'm sure they're up to something," Kyle stated.

"Agreed."

Other members of the team arrived, putting a halt to their conversation.

Phillipa greeted her team, then lapsed into case assignments and updates.

"I'm still working on the Helena Rossi case," she stated. "At this time, I don't have anything to report. I'm still following up on leads."

"It's good you were able to find a lead," one team member, Alice, said. "The last detective didn't find anything."

"Are you familiar with the case?" Phillipa asked.

"I assisted the last detective."

"Let's talk after the meeting. I'd like to hear your thoughts."

The woman smiled. "Sure."

She needed someone familiar with the case who had fresh eyes. Alice was a retired homicide detective who'd been with CMPD for over twenty years. She now volunteered her time with CCU.

After the meeting, Phillipa and Alice retreated to her office, where she gave Alice a quick update on the current investigation.

The woman sat there with her mouth open in shock. "Let me make sure I'm understanding this. Helena Rossi was born Clara Davis, who supposedly died in 2006?"

"Yes."

"Her best friend was abducted along with Clara. The friend was found murdered—Clara's body was found a few months later in Atlanta. But you believe it wasn't really her. She wanted someone to believe she'd died."

"That's the sum of it," Phillipa said.

"She was running," Alice stated. "The real question is why. If you find the answer to that, it will lead you to the perp."

"Kyle and I figure she was there when her friend was killed."

"If she was, then why would the shooter wait to kill her, too?"

"She got away somehow?" Phillipa offered. "Alice,

I feel like this goes deeper than that. It's possible she escaped, but why not go to the police?"

"Because she'd be labeled a snitch," Alice responded. "She wasn't going to do that, but maybe the perp didn't know it."

"You were working in Homicide when Helena was killed. I know the case didn't cross your desk, but do you remember if anything stuck out to you back then?"

"I felt like her background was too vague. Most people have a friend from their childhood. Her only real friend was Paula Johnson. She had a couple of people from her church whom Helena seemed close to—that was it. Now I understand why."

Alice read over a few notes. "It's eerie that Helena died in a similar way as Myra Rowland. I'd be tempted to say they were killed by the same person, but different guns. This is just my opinion, but it's almost like the way she was shot was supposed to send some sort of message."

"I felt the same way about the body being placed at the gazebo," Phillipa said. "It doesn't seem random to me."

"I agree," Alice said.

They spent the next hour going over Helena's murder book.

"Was Alice able to help?" Kyle asked at the end of the day as they were heading out to their cars.

"Not really," Phillipa responded. "I hope I didn't offend you by asking her to take a look."

"You didn't," he assured her. "Alice knows her stuff."

Kyle didn't mind anyone helping with Helena's case. Especially if it brought them closer to a suspect.

He made sure Phillipa was safely in her vehicle before walking to his own.

Phillipa was back to her normal self, and Kyle enjoyed seeing this side of her. Some of the other team members commented on how relaxed she seemed lately. It was even reflected in her hairstyle—she wore it loose and carefree rather than pulled back.

Sitting in his car, Kyle suddenly felt the hair on his arms stand to attention.

He didn't glance around; instead, he pretended not to notice. But without moving his head, he allowed his eyes to dart around, searching to see if he could find whoever was watching him.

I'm going to find you, he vowed.

Kyle drove out of the parking lot of the precinct slowly. Nothing and no one stood out to him. It had to be someone who could blend in easily. Kyle wasn't afraid or deterred. If anything, it motivated him more.

He waited until he was home before calling Phillipa.

"I'm pretty sure someone was watching me when I left the precinct. Nothing stood out though."

"Do you think you were followed home?" she asked.

"Naw," he responded. "I made sure I didn't have a tail."

"What if it was the same person who broke into your house? They would already have the address."

"My cameras are installed. I checked the streets before I called you. I didn't see anything out of the ordinary."

They talked a few minutes more before ending the call.

Smiling, Kyle laid his phone on the kitchen counter. He liked the tone of his relationship with Phillipa and the direction in which it was going. He felt she was beginning to trust him again.

It was an answer to his prayer concerning her. Well, the first part of it anyway.

Kyle was grateful, nonetheless.

Phillipa had accepted his invitation to his mother's birthday dinner. He was looking forward to spending another evening with her—one that had nothing to do with work. They both needed to balance the hours they'd put in on cold cases with some laughter. He'd known a couple of detectives over the years who'd burned out quickly because they didn't have the bandwidth to handle the caseload.

He admired Phillipa's dedication to ensuring her team kept a balanced caseload. She preferred to assign cases to the detectives who specialized in that case type versus assigning to whoever was on duty. She was proving to be a wonderful addition to CCU.

Kyle spent the rest of the evening making notes in preparation for his interview with the Robbery Division, which was in two days. He'd been advised that in addition to passing the promotional exam, he should be prepared to offer examples to the panel of how he was already performing some of the same important supervisory responsibilities as sergeants.

He'd devoted a lot of time to passing the exam and preparing for this interview. Kyle prayed it would pay off in the form of a job offer.

Chapter Nineteen

"This is really nice," Phillipa said, her eyes bouncing around the private room in the back of an Italian restaurant. The walls were draped in rich but soothing jewel tones. Round tables draped in white and decorated with colorful floral centerpieces were arranged neatly around the room.

"Jon picked it," Kyle responded as he escorted her into the private dining room. "My mom loves Italian food. She has no idea that Jon and I are gifting her with a week in Italy. She and Dad were planning to visit there before he got sick."

"It's a beautiful birthday gift."

They sat down at a reserved table.

When Paula joined them, Phillipa greeted her politely. She could tell Kyle wasn't happy that she'd been seated with them.

Jon came to sit between Kyle and Paula.

Paula glanced between her and Kyle. "You two are looking really chummy," she said. "Tell me...are there wedding bells in your future?"

Kyle ignored her question.

Jon whispered something in Paula's ear, which apparently, she didn't like, judging from the sharp glare she shot in his direction.

"Your mother looks stunning," Phillipa whispered to Kyle when Amelie made her grand entrance fifteen minutes later on the arm of Pastor Brady.

"I guess they're making it official," Paula said.

"There you go making assumptions again," Kyle responded. "This is how rumors get started."

"I know that they've gone out a couple of times," she began.

Kyle cut her off by saying, "They're friends, Paula. Until they say otherwise, you should just leave it alone."

She looked over at Jon. "Aren't you going to come to my defense? You know I didn't mean any harm."

"I happen to agree with my brother."

Paula pushed away from the table. "Excuse me, please," she said before walking briskly toward the restrooms outside of the room.

"Don't you think you were a little hard on her?" Phillipa asked.

Kyle shook his head. "My mother's business is her own."

"I agree," Jon said.

As soon as Amelie was seated, servers began bringing the food out. Asparagus spears wrapped in prosciutto, balsamic-glazed *cipollini* onions and sautéed beef tips were served as an appetizer.

While they dined, Phillipa saw familiar glimpses of Kyle's wonderful sense of humor. They laughed throughout their meal, and she couldn't deny how much she really enjoyed spending time with him.

He caught her watching him and flashed a grin, which caused a shudder to pass through her.

Phillipa leaned over and said, "Miss Amelie looks happy. She even has a glow about her."

"I'm saying this to you only. I'm pretty sure that glow you're seeing is because of Pastor Brady. She's finally agreed to let him court her properly. Her words, not mine."

"Oh, wow…" She looked at Kyle. "I'm really thrilled for your mother."

"Me, too. She deserves so much more than what Jon and I could ever give her." He cleared his throat, then continued. "The reason I didn't come to California was because I felt you deserved more than I could give you. I thought you'd found it with Raya's father."

"I tried," Phillipa said. "But I recognized almost immediately that I'd made a mistake rushing into marriage with Gary. I didn't want to hurt him, so I tried to make it work. The day I was going to talk to him about taking time apart, I found out I was pregnant."

"So you decided to stay with him," Kyle interjected.

"I did," she confirmed. "I really wanted the marriage to work, but I wasn't in love with Gary. He's a wonderful person, but I think we would've made better friends than man and wife. I thought maybe once I had Raya, my feelings would change. I hoped they would anyway."

Phillipa took a sip of water. "We stayed together until Raya was eight. We had a nice birthday party for her, and that night, Gary asked for a divorce. I had to admit that I didn't see it coming, but I was relieved. It didn't take him long to find someone who could really love him—they're getting married next month."

"How do you feel about it?"

"I hope he'll be happy," she responded. "He deserves it."

"You said I was to blame for the failure of your marriage."

She shook her head. "I never should've said that to you because it wasn't your fault. It was mine. I wanted to love him, but I couldn't."

"If you don't mind my asking… Why was it so hard for you to love him?" Kyle inquired.

"Because of you."

"I'm not sure what you mean by that."

"You were the love of my life, Kyle. I felt like you were the other half of me. When things ended between us… I was broken. A huge chunk of me was missing, and that included my heart."

"I felt the same way," he told her. "You have no idea how many times I kicked myself for calling off the engagement. When I heard you were getting married… Well, I'll just say I had a bad time of it."

"I suppose if I hadn't left town like I did, maybe things would've turned out differently."

"I believe they would have," Kyle stated. "We wouldn't have had so much tension between us." He smiled. "C'mon, let's dance," he said, rising to his feet. "I really like this song."

Phillipa allowed him to take her by the hand and lead her to the dance floor. They were soon joined by friends and family.

They danced through the next three songs. Then, laughing, she allowed him to walk her from the dance floor to a nearby bar. She wanted a bottle of water.

"I can't remember the last time I danced like that," Phillipa said. "This was so much fun. I don't know about you, but it's been a while since I've danced like this."

"It's been a while for me as well. I see you still have some moves."

"I don't know about that," she responded with a short laugh. "I had to watch YouTube to see what people are doing these days."

"The twins are always showing me the latest dance moves," Kyle said. "That's my little secret. I never thought of watching YouTube."

They laughed as they walked outside to take in some fresh air.

She looked up at the sky. "It's so beautiful out here."

"Yes, it is," Kyle responded.

When her gaze turned to him, Phillipa thought she saw a whisper of something inviting in Kyle's eyes. It was a look that said he wouldn't mind a kiss. She caught her breath as he half bent down toward her.

Phillipa's chest filled with the anticipation, and then he kissed her.

"I've wanted to do that all evening," Kyle whispered in her ear.

She drew his face to hers in a renewed embrace. "Kiss me again," Phillipa replied, lifting her mouth to accept another gentle kiss. Her emotions whirled, blood pounded, leapt from her heart and made her knees tremble. She savored every moment.

And Phillipa realized in that moment that she could never escape her feelings for him.

Bethany was curled up on the sofa in the family room when Phillipa got home. "Mom, are you feeling any better?"

Her mother had had a migraine headache earlier,

which was why she'd had to miss the birthday dinner for Amelie.

"The meds finally kicked in," she responded as she shifted her position on the sofa. Bethany adjusted the plush throw covering her. "Did you have a good time?"

"I did. It was a very nice party for his mom. You should've seen Miss Amelie. She looked really beautiful. I told her that you weren't feeling well."

"Did she come with Pastor Brady?"

"Yes, she did. How did you know about that?" Phillipa asked.

"Amelie and I are friends. We *talk*."

"Oh…"

"What? You think that all Amelie and I talk about is you and Kyle? Well, we actually have lives, hon."

Phillipa laughed. "Thanks for setting me straight."

"Speaking of Kyle… He picked you up tonight, didn't he?" Bethany asked.

She nodded. "He did." Phillipa knew the direction where this conversation was going. For once, she didn't mind. She needed to talk to someone about her warring emotions.

"So, you were his date?"

"I'm not sure I'd call it that," Phillipa responded. "We're not putting a label on anything."

"Did you kiss him?"

Phillipa's eyebrows rose in surprise. "Mom…"

"Well, did you?" Bethany asked.

"We kissed but it wasn't the first time. Kyle kissed me once while we were at work."

"Did you enjoy it?"

She gave an embarrassed chuckle. "I can't believe you're asking me this. I'm a grown woman."

"No matter how old you get, you will always be my little girl. My baby," Bethany stated. She patted the empty space beside her. "Now share… I want the details."

"Kissing him was nice," Phillipa said. "Both times. It made me realize just how much I've missed the feel of his lips on mine. Kyle's always been a good kisser."

Bethany sat there grinning. "I haven't seen you like this in a long time."

"I feel like I'm in high school all over again. I really enjoyed being with Kyle tonight. There wasn't any pressure because it wasn't a date. Still, it was nice. We danced, laughed and just had fun."

"Do you think you'll be seeing more of Kyle outside of work?"

"I don't know," Phillipa responded. "We work in the same unit and I'm his supervisor. It could be problematic. We'd have to disclose our relationship and one of us would have to transfer. I don't have any intention of leaving CCU."

"Perhaps Kyle will consider transferring."

"I don't know," she said. "We're not in a space to even have that conversation."

"Yet tonight was a huge step for you and Kyle," Bethany said.

"Yes, it was, and honestly, I don't have any regrets."

"You shouldn't. Just enjoy the now."

"I intend to do just that, Mom." Phillipa got up. "I'm going to bed. Do you need anything?"

"I'm good. I'm going to wait up for your father."

"He's out late," Phillipa said.

"He went out a short time ago to pick up some tea I've been wanting."

"You sure you're okay?"

Bethany nodded. "I'm fine, hon."

Phillipa went upstairs. She checked on Raya, who had chosen to stay home with her grandmother.

She found her daughter watching television in the loft.

"Why are you still up?" Phillipa asked. "It's almost midnight."

"I was waiting for you," Raya responded. She stretched and yawned. "Did you have fun?"

"I had a great time."

"I'm glad." Raya yawned a second time. "I hope Miss Amelie had a good birthday. She's a real nice lady."

"Why don't you go to bed, sweetie?" Phillipa said. She gave one of Raya's braids a gentle tug.

"I need to check on Grandma."

"She's feeling much better. I just left her in the family room."

Raya stood up and turned off the television. "That's good. I guess I'll go to bed. See you in the morning."

Phillipa walked her to her bedroom. "Goodnight, sweetie."

"G'night. Love you."

She walked down the hall to her room.

Phillipa could still feel the heat from Kyle's kiss. She wanted more of his kisses, but she wouldn't risk it. She had to navigate around her team as a professional. Besides, she had no idea how things would go from here with Kyle.

One thing was for sure—she couldn't allow him to become a distraction. They had too much important work to do.

Two weeks passed and nothing new on Helena's investigation. Kyle still held onto hope for a lead to manifest.

He took a phone call, then sent an email to Phillipa

requesting a meeting. She was currently in a conference room with the CCU reviewers.

Minutes later, he received a response to his email.

Sure. I can meet with you at 1:30. See you then.

A smile tugged at his lips. Kyle had persuaded his captain to allow him to tell Phillipa about the new position. He couldn't wait to see the expression on her face when he shared his news with her.

His eyes traveled to the clock on the wall near his desk. It was almost noon.

Kyle decided to grab something to eat before meeting with Phillipa.

He stood to his feet, grabbed his keys and headed to his cruiser.

"Hey, what's going on?" Phillipa asked when Kyle entered her office at approximately one-thirty.

He sat down, then said, "I interviewed for a position with the Robbery Division. I was notified earlier that I got the job."

"Congratulations," she murmured. "I have to admit that I had no idea that you wanted to leave the department."

"I thought about this a lot and I think it's for the best."

"I guess I thought we were getting along much better."

"Phillipa, the reason I don't want to stay in CCU is because I want to date you. I'm transferring to Robbery as a sergeant. We won't have to worry about any type of office scandal breaking out. I didn't want things to become awkward for you."

She broke into a smile. "You've been busy, I see. However, I haven't agreed to go out with you."

He grinned. "I was waiting before I asked you... Phillipa, I'd really like for us to give it another try."

"Even though I'm still dealing with some issues?"

"We can sort through them together. Especially if they involve me."

"Are you sure about this? I have Raya now. I don't want to bring anyone around her if they're not going to be in my life for a significant period of time."

"I understand," he responded. "Trust me when I say that I've had more than enough time to figure out what I want. But I'm not trying to rush into anything until you're ready."

"I still have a case to solve."

"I know," he responded. "That will remain the priority." Kyle met her gaze. "Can I start seeing you socially?"

"I'd like that...once you start working in Robbery," she said with a smile. "Until then, we keep it professional, and we focus on Helena."

"Agreed," Kyle replied. "I guess I'd better get back to work. I want to try and close as many of my cases as possible before I leave."

"I'll take over the ones you don't get a chance to close. Just make sure I have detailed summaries of everything you've done."

"Will do," he stated.

After Kyle left, Phillipa sat at her desk sorting out her feelings. She was truly happy for him. The move to Robbery was a promotion, putting him in the same rank as her. But she couldn't deny that she'd miss working with him in CCU.

On the other hand, she'd see more of him socially. Phillipa was a bit nervous about the idea of dating Kyle after all these years, but she opted to keep an open mind. This was a second chance at love, and she didn't want to ruin it by worrying about the future.

Chapter Twenty

Phillipa checked her reflection in the mirror while she waited for Kyle to arrive. They were celebrating his first day in the new unit.

"You look beautiful," Raya said.

Dressed in a black sweater dress with a rose gold belt and black leather booties, she sat down on the edge of the bed. "How do you feel about me seeing Kyle?"

"He's nice. I like him."

"So, you're really okay with this?"

Raya nodded. "You've asked me this, like, four times."

"I know how upset you got when you found out your dad was getting married."

"I'm starting to be okay with it." She looked up at her mother. "Are you gonna marry Mr. Kyle?"

"No, we're a long way from that," Phillipa said.

"You'll tell me when you start thinking about it?"

"I promise."

Kyle arrived on time and they were soon on their way to the restaurant.

Phillipa smiled to herself, reassured that her daughter was at least going to be honest with her about her feelings where she and Kyle were concerned. That was the best she could hope for.

But at the restaurant, the nerves she'd tried hard to bury must have surfaced because Kyle asked, "Phillipa, what's wrong?"

"I'm not quite sure I'm ready for this…you and me."

"You still don't completely trust me with your heart," he stated.

"I want to, Kyle, but it's a process."

"I understand. I'm not trying to rush you into a relationship. I think it's best that we take our time."

Smiling, she said, "You amaze me."

"Why do you say that?"

"You're so easygoing and understanding. I'm over here freaking out inside because I spent so many years angry with you—it's hard to think of you as something more than the man who broke my heart. I just have to find a way to bury the past for good."

"Like you said…it's a process, and I'm a very patient man."

The server brought their food. But Phillipa didn't care to swirl strings of pasta around a fork when her gaze could be held by Kyle's, and her mouth didn't want to be busy eating when they could be talking. The restaurant suddenly became too noisy, too busy, and all the distractions were unwelcome. She wanted to shut out any awareness of everything else—she just wanted it to be the two of them.

"How's your food?" Kyle asked.

"It's delicious," she responded. "They just give you so much of it. I'm going to have to take half of it home with me."

The waiter came over with a bottle of champagne and poured two glasses.

"You ordered champagne?" Phillipa normally didn't touch anything with alcohol in it.

Kyle nodded. "It's nonalcoholic, and we have something to celebrate."

"What is that?" she asked.

"Friendship."

"You mean us?"

"That's what you want, right? I told you that I wouldn't pressure you with the demands of a relationship. When you're ready for something more, you'll let me know."

Phillipa instantly relaxed. This was one of the reasons she loved Kyle. He was always so thoughtful and considerate.

They made easy conversation as they finished off their meals. Then Kyle paid the check, and they left the restaurant.

"You were serious about taking half of your food home," he said.

"I couldn't eat all of it."

On the way to the car, Phillipa suddenly stopped in her tracks. "Kyle…"

"Huh?"

"Check out the couple going into that restaurant across the street."

His eyes followed the direction of her gaze. "That's Paula and Miller."

"Exactly," she responded. "I wonder how those two know each other—and how long they've been connected."

Phillipa took several quick photographs.

"I'd say that Helena's case just took an interesting turn," Kyle stated.

"I'm inclined to believe you. It's not a coincidence. It can't be."

They sat inside his car and waited.

"I want to see where they go after dinner," Phillipa said.

"Do you think...?" Kyle asked.

"I do," she responded. "They're involved. Remember, Miller told us that he didn't come to Charlotte often. So I have to wonder how he met Paula. Especially since he claimed not to know anything about Helena."

"Are you in a hurry to get home?"

"Not at all," Phillipa responded. "I'd like to hang out here and talk to you."

He grinned. "I'd like that, too."

"I have a strong feeling that we've found our missing piece of the puzzle," Phillipa said.

"I think so, too."

An hour later, Paula and Miller walked out holding hands.

"Ooh, yeah..." Phillipa murmured.

They followed Miller's car to Paula's house, where Phillipa took more pictures when the couple emerged from the car and went inside.

"What are you thinking?" he asked.

"What if Miller knew about Helena before we told him?" Phillipa said. "That would explain some of his anger. We definitely have to have a conversation with the two of them."

Kyle seemed to be still pondering Phillipa's question. "And if he did know about Helena...how long has he known?"

"That was my next question."

"Paula told you about the degree in Clara's name," he said. "She could have told Miller as well."

Frowning, Phillipa responded, "We're missing a piece in that theory. How did she connect with Miller? Do you think she found out about Myra somehow?"

"I wouldn't put it past her to snoop to try to find dirt on Helena. Especially since she was after the woman's husband."

"So, you think Paula set things in motion."

"It makes sense," Kyle responded. "She has a motive. She wanted Jon for herself. And remember how she kept asking us for information on the case."

"But do you think she shot Helena?"

"She's ruthless enough, but no," Kyle responded. "More likely Miller for the shooting. He's muscular and strong enough to carry a body to the gazebo. I think they're in this together."

Phillipa nodded. "We'll find out soon enough."

The next day, an officer knocked on Phillipa's door and said, "She's in Room One."

"Thanks." She looked at Kyle, who came over from his unit to the interrogation room. "Hopefully Paula will be a little more forthcoming this time."

"Only after you force her hand, most likely," he responded.

Phillipa pushed away from her desk and stood up. "Miller should be arriving in fifteen minutes."

"I'd like to sit in on both interviews," Kyle stated.

"As long as you let me do the talking."

He agreed, and Paula looked up when she and Kyle walked in.

"Why am I here?" she demanded. "I've told you everything I know."

"I don't believe that's true," Phillipa responded. "We need you to clear up a few things for us."

"I'll certainly do what I can."

Phillipa decided to get straight to the point. "How long have you known Miller Rowland?"

"Who?"

"Miller Rowland."

"I'm sorry... I don't know anyone by that name," Paula stated as she averted her gaze.

Not in the mood for lies, Phillipa placed a photograph in front of her. "Who is the man you had dinner with last night?"

Paula looked at Kyle and asked, "Can you please tell me what this is about?"

"Sergeant Stevenson asked you a question."

"Where did you get these pictures?" Paula asked. "Are you having me followed?"

Phillipa didn't respond.

Paula sent her a sharp glare before saying, "Fine. His name is Miller Rowland and he's a friend. We get together whenever he comes to town. Kyle, I hope you won't say anything to your brother."

"Why did you deny knowing Miller?" Phillipa questioned.

"Because I didn't want Jon to find out. There's nothing serious between Miller and me."

Phillipa repeated her original question. "How long have you known him?"

"A few years. I don't remember how long, but it's been a while." Paula glanced from Phillipa to Kyle. "Is someone gonna tell me what's going on? Why are you suddenly so interested in my personal life?"

"How did you meet Miller?"

"I met him at a medical function with Helena. Jon was the keynote speaker."

"Did you know my sister-in-law was pregnant when she died?" Kyle blurted.

Paula's sharp glance shot to him. She shook her head. "She wasn't pregnant."

"Yes, she was," Phillipa responded.

"She must not have known at the time because I'm sure Helena would've told me."

"With you being her best friend and all," Phillipa remarked. "Helena found out six weeks before she died."

"Noooo…" Paula shook her head again, then burst into tears. "Oh, nooo…"

Handing her a tissue, Phillipa said, "You've been carrying this burden for twelve years. Why don't you tell us what happened to Helena?"

"If you care anything for my brother," Kyle said, "you'll tell the truth, Paula."

"Miller must be behind her death," she said after a moment.

"Go on…" Phillipa prompted.

"I went with Helena to hear Jon speak. Miller was there—he approached us, and he addressed Helena as Clara. I noticed how shocked he seemed that she was alive. He told her that she was supposed to be dead. Helena ran off. I went after her."

"What happened?"

"She was scared—I'd never seen her like that. Helena started crying, so I gave her a pill to calm her nerves. I had no idea why she was so upset."

Kyle looked over at Phillipa, an unreadable expression on his face.

"Miller asked for my phone number later that evening. He's very attractive and I wasn't dating anyone. I didn't see any harm in it. Now I feel like I was manipulated. He used me to get to Helena. I don't know why I didn't see it before."

"What motive would he have for wanting to hurt Helena?" Phillipa asked.

"I…"

She laid down her pen. "Paula, I'm not in the mood for games. I want the truth."

"I'm not lying!" she screamed.

"Did Miller ever mention Myra Rowland?" Phillipa asked.

"She was his twin," Paula answered. "She died years ago."

"But he's never mentioned Clara Davis to you?"

"If he did, I don't remember."

"That's interesting," Phillipa said. "You remembered the name Clara on a degree in Helena's possession."

"Is that the same person?"

"It is," she responded. "C'mon, Paula…stop lying to us. You know all about Clara Davis."

"All right…" The woman sighed. "I admit my interest was piqued when Miller confronted Helena, so I did some research. Miller told me about his sister and Clara—he was so angry. He told me that Helena was really Clara and that he was going to make her pay. I didn't ask no questions."

"When Helena went missing, didn't you get suspicious?" Phillipa inquired.

"I think I was too afraid to ask any questions."

"But you didn't have a problem seeing the man all these years—the man who may have killed your best friend."

"I didn't want to believe that Miller had anything to do with something so horrible." She played with her hands. "I just put it out of my head."

"Paula, I don't think you're telling me everything."

She started to cry. "I don't want to have anything to do with this. You're gonna get me killed."

"Why do you say that?"

"I'm afraid of Miller. If I tell you what I know, he'll kill me. I need protection."

"If you talk to us now, we can arrest him."

"The truth is that I've suspected for years that Miller killed Helena, but like I said… I was afraid of him. I didn't have anything to do with her death. Kyle, you know how much I detest guns after what happened to my brother. The reason I kept asking about the case was because I was hoping that you would've picked him up by now."

"If you'd told us about him twelve years ago, Miller would've already been tried and put in prison," Kyle interjected.

"I'm sorry." Paula wiped her face. "What happens now?"

"You tell us the truth," Phillipa said.

"I've told you all I know. The person you're looking for is Miller. You should catch him before he leaves town."

Phillipa placed a hand on Kyle's arm. "Why don't you take a break?"

"I'm fine." He looked at Paula. "There's something else I want to know… Someone broke into my house and went through a stack of files on my desk. This person used a key, and they most likely knew I didn't have cameras installed."

"Miller kept pressing me to find out what you knew. I took some files along with Helena's but I only made a copy of her file."

"I should've known it was you."

"Kyle, all I wanted to do was protect Jon…"

"No, you wanted him for yourself—only, he never got over losing Helena."

"Once Jon hears the truth, his feelings will change," Paula uttered. "You don't know how much I wanted to tell him the truth about his wife. I couldn't because I didn't want to implicate myself."

Kyle shrugged. "Now he'll hear all about your actions, too."

"I can explain everything to Jon."

Kyle shook his head. "My brother won't have anything to do with you. I can guarantee that."

Chapter Twenty-One

Phillipa and Kyle walked out of the interrogation room.

"She knows exactly what happened to Helena," Phillipa said. "I'm sure of it."

He nodded in agreement. "I can't believe after all this time… Paula knew who was responsible and she let Jon… That woman is sick."

"I have to admit, I never suspected her of anything other than a not-very-good friend to Helena."

"Same here," Kyle muttered. "We were right about Paula. We just didn't know just how deep her betrayal went."

"Now, I'm about to go into this room and talk to Miller. I'm pretty sure I'm going to have to drag a confession out of him."

"He might surprise you," Kyle responded. "Miller's arrogant and he likes to be in control. If he senses that you're on to him, he'll try to control the narrative."

"We're about to find out." Phillipa walked into the interrogation room where Miller sat waiting.

He was tapping his fingers on the table impatiently. "I came here before of my own accord. I thought I'd answered all your questions, Sergeant Stevenson. Why did you want to see me and how did you know I was even in town? Are you having me followed?"

Instead of answering his queries, Phillipa said, "When I asked if you'd heard of Helena Rossi, you lied to me. It appears you've known all along that Clara Davis and Helena Rossi were the same person."

He didn't respond.

"I just finished talking to a friend of yours," Phillipa stated.

"What friend?"

"Paula Johnson. Are you going to deny that you know her as well?"

Miller seemed to realize there was no point in lying. He shrugged in nonchalance and said, "I guess she told you everything. Since she had so much to say, did Paula also tell you that all this started because of her."

"What do you mean by that?" Phillipa asked.

"She was the one who came to me. She wanted my help in getting rid of Clara."

"Why don't you start from the beginning?"

"My mother was contacted in 2008 by Paula. She was asking about Clara Davis. I got involved because it really upset my mom and I wanted to know what it was all about. Paula sent me a picture of Helena. I thought she'd been murdered, too, but then I see her alive and well, living her best life while my family and I grieved the loss of Myra. Paula told me that Clara had actually confessed to killing my sister."

"And you believed her?"

"I did. I didn't see why she had any reason to lie about something like that."

"Maybe it was because she wanted Helena's husband," Phillipa said.

Miller shrugged. "I bet Paula told you all this was my idea."

Nodding, Phillipa replied, "She blamed you for everything."

He shook his head. "She's lying. Paula set all this up from the moment she found Clara's degree," Miller said. "We spent a year planning what would happen. She even arranged for me to be at a fundraiser she was attending with Clara so I could confront her."

His expression changed to one of disgust. "When I saw her, Clara had the nerve to offer me money. As if that would bring my family closure. All it did was make me angrier. That woman deserved to die."

"So, you decided to act as her punisher. Why not go to the police?"

"Because I didn't want Clara's husband's money to get her off. You should've seen the way she lied to my face. She kept saying that my sister pulled a gun on her. She said Myra's death was an accident. Then she started begging for forgiveness. Told me she was a different person now. She showed me pictures of her children and her husband—I didn't care. My sister will never have any of those things."

"Did she tell you that she was pregnant?" Phillipa asked.

"Yeah, but I didn't care," he responded with another shrug. "I don't regret shooting her or Savage. All this time, I thought he was the one who'd murdered Myra. Don't matter though. He deserved to be killed anyway." Miller stared at her coldly. "Clara was already dead. I just made sure she stayed dead."

"You may think this makes you a better person, but it doesn't," Phillipa said.

Miller didn't show an ounce of remorse. "I avenged my sister. That's all I care about."

She got up and walked over to the door to signal for an officer to join her.

Phillipa wondered if he was even aware that he'd confessed to another murder. Savage's murder was still unsolved. She planned to call Detective Bancroft to update him after having Miller charged and booked.

Miller's full-blown anger and bitterness toward Helena forced Phillipa to reflect on her own emotions, but now wasn't the time for reflecting. They finally had the answers they'd been looking for—and they had not only one suspect, but two.

Phillipa walked out behind Miller and the police office.

Kyle met her in the hallway. "You did it."

"We did it," she responded. "Now I've got to call the prosecutor, but I'll catch up with you later."

"Congratulations," he said.

Phillipa smiled. "Back at you."

Just then, Paula was escorted out of the other room in handcuffs. Tears rolled down her cheeks. She glowered at Phillipa, then said, "I wish you'd never come back here. You've ruined my life."

"No, you did that a long time ago. You lie without remorse...now it's time for you to pay for your actions."

"I didn't do anything! It was all Miller."

"I don't believe you," Phillipa responded.

She didn't believe a word out of Paula's mouth. She felt Miller's version of events was the truth. There was one question that remained on her mind: Did Helena kill Myra?

* * *

An hour later, Phillipa sought out Kyle. She found him in his new office.

"I just got off the phone with the district attorney. They're going to charge Miller with two counts of first-degree murder. One for Helena and the other for the baby she was carrying. She said the prosecutor in Miami is looking to charge him with Savage's shooting. Paula's being charged as well in Helena's murder. She's being charged with criminal conspiracy to commit murder, solicitation of murder and hindering prosecution in the murder."

"What a mess," Kyle uttered. "Clara killed her best friend, then left to start a new life as Helena. I guess 'what goes around comes around' is a true statement. Poor woman was then murdered by another best friend."

"The thing is that we don't really know if she killed Myra. There's no evidence—I believe Paula told Miller that because she knew he'd want revenge."

"Something happened between the two girls," Kyle said. "Helena told Miller that Myra was the one with the gun. Maybe they fought over it and it went off. It might have been an accident. Maybe that's why she asked him to forgive her."

"Or she could've witnessed Savage killing Myra and run," Phillipa suggested. "Maybe Helena felt guilty because she didn't do anything to save her friend."

"The sad thing is we will never know what really happened. How in the world do we explain all this to Jon?"

"I've been thinking about that… None of this is going to be easy for him to accept. We're going to have to tell him everything because it's all going to come out during the trial. And to get his permission for the DNA test. The prosecutor wants proof that the two women are one and the same."

"The girls are going to be devastated when they hear about Paula's part in their mother's death." Kyle shook his head sadly. "They loved Paula."

"I'm sorry about that. I didn't care for the woman, but I never thought she had anything to do with Helena's death."

"I never cared for Paula, either," Kyle began, "but to spare my family more pain, I'd rather have been wrong about her. I almost hope that Miller is lying about her part in this."

"I don't think he is," Phillipa said. "I've secured a warrant to serve on her cell phone provider. We're asking for her phone history going back to 2008. We'll know for sure once we review her records."

The anguish he must've felt showed in his eyes. Phillipa yearned to reach out and comfort him. She understood his need to protect his brother and nieces, but there was no way to shield them from the truth.

She sent up a silent prayer asking God to give the Rossi family strength to endure what would come next.

Kyle sat at his desk feeling the weight of all they'd learned. A part of him wished he hadn't persisted in finding Helena's killer because he never wanted to cause more hurt to Jon and the girls.

Phillipa was right. It couldn't be avoided. He only wished he didn't have to tell his brother that Helena may have killed someone.

Kyle released a long sigh as he considered the close relationship between Paula and the twins. But as a family, they would get through this.

His thoughts were interrupted when a member of his new team came to his office to brief him on an armed robbery investigation.

After the detective left, Kyle's troubled thoughts returned. He decided not to dwell on them now, pushing them away.

He picked up the official case summary of a carjacking investigation to review. The perp had been apprehended and booked earlier.

Next, Kyle responded to several emails that required his attention. If he stayed busy, he wouldn't have to think about the Pandora's box he'd insisted on opening. He felt responsible for having to break Jon's heart all over again.

"Kelsey Brown is here to see you, Sergeant Stevenson," an officer announced when Phillipa walked out of Captain Peters' office.

"Take her to Interview Room One, please," she said. "Oh, and ask Sergeant Rossi to join me?"

"Yes, ma'am."

He met her outside the interview room a moment later. "Do you have any idea why she's here?"

Phillipa shook her head. "I guess we'll learn now." She studied the woman seated on the other side of a speckled white rectangle-shaped table. Kelsey Brown looked familiar to her, but she was sure they'd never met.

"I'm Sergeant Phillipa Stevenson," she said, walking into the room. "And this is Sergeant Kyle Rossi."

"I can't live with this secret anymore," Kelsey blurted without preamble. "It's time the truth came out about everything."

Phillipa glanced over at Kyle, then back at Kelsey. "The truth about what?" she asked.

"After you called me, I knew I had to tell you about Clara and Myra. I came to the station once before. I saw you leave, so I followed you. You went to a park."

Phillipa remembered that day—it was the day she felt someone watching her.

"When I saw you sitting in the gazebo…it reminded me of one in Miami. It was near Clara's house. The three of us used to sit there for hours, talking about our plans for the future. Seeing you there just shook me to my core. I figured I'd just leave things alone."

Phillipa eyed Kelsey. "Helena Rossi's body was found in that very gazebo."

Kelsey's eyes grew wide, and her expression was one of surprise. "I didn't know that." She swallowed hard before saying, "You asked me on the phone that day if I knew Helena. I didn't tell you then, but the answer is yes. I'm sure you've already figured out that she was born Clara Davis."

"Yes. What I'd like to know is why do you think she changed her name."

"I can tell you that. Back then, we thought it was cool to hang with Savage and his boys," Kelsey said. "Savage and Clara were involved, but then he started messing around with Myra. I told her to leave him alone. Myra wouldn't listen. She wanted him for herself. See…he'd bought Clara a car. Myra…she wanted one, too. Anyway, Clara found them together one day, and the girls had a fight. Savage broke it up. He told them that he was done with both of them. He told them that he was having a baby with this other girl, and she was the one he wanted to be with."

Phillipa let that sink in. "So, he basically dumped them both."

Kelsey nodded. "After that, Myra and Clara stopped talking. We weren't the three musketeers anymore. Each one kept trying to get me to pick a side. I got tired of being in the middle, so I told them we needed to meet up and talk things out."

"So, you were *there* that day?" Phillipa asked.

Kelsey nodded. "We met and things started off fine. Clara apologized and wanted to move past the drama, but not Myra. She refused to let it go. It got so bad between them that Clara decided it was time to walk away for good. That's when Myra pulled a gun on Clara."

"Did Clara have a gun?" Kyle asked.

"Yeah… We all carried, but she never took hers out."

Phillipa stole a quick peek at Kyle before asking, "So, what happened?"

"I tried to get Myra to calm down, but she was so angry. She wasn't listening to anything I said. We'd been best friends since we were in elementary school, the three of us, but it was suddenly as if she hated Clara… I'd never seen her like that." Kelsey's voice shook as she continued, "Clara was leaving and then I saw Myra point the gun at her—I don't even remember getting mine, but all I knew was that I had to stop Myra. I pulled the trigger…" Tears ran down her face. "Clara… She wasn't just my friend. She was family. My cousin. Elijah Davis was my dad—everyone tried to keep quiet about it because he was married at the time and had a family. He'd met my mom when he came to Miami for a visit. Clara's mama was the only one who claimed me. She made sure Clara and I had a relationship."

Phillipa stared at her. "You were at her wedding. I saw you there."

Kelsey nodded.

"So, you're telling me that you killed Myra."

She started to sob. "I didn't want to kill her, but I couldn't just let her shoot Clara in the back. After I shot Myra, we made it look as if she and Clara had been kidnapped. Savage and I were cousins on my mama's side. He had one of his boys get rid of Myra's body and had another drive Clara to Atlanta. I knew my dad and his brother—Clara's father—would help us. I waited a couple months before taking the bus to Virginia. After her wedding, Clara and I decided it was best not to see each other again."

"So, you never spoke after that?"

"Only once," Kelsey stated. "She called me in a panic to tell me that Miller knew she was alive. They were at a conference or something. She wanted to run away but I told her to talk to her husband. To tell him the truth. I was sure he loved her enough to protect her. I called her a couple days later. I never got an answer, so I drove to Charlotte and went by the house. I didn't stop because I saw the police. I read in the newspaper that she'd been killed."

"Miller is in custody for her murder," Phillipa announced.

Kelsey nodded. "I had a feeling it was him. But you see… I couldn't say anything to you without implicating myself." She eyed Phillipa. "What happens to me now?"

"You will have to face charges in Miami. Tell them what happened."

"I never set out to kill anyone. I just wanted my cousin

and my friend to stop fighting. I never thought Myra would be angry enough to want Clara dead…"

"I understand," Phillipa said. "But all this would've been easier to sort out if you'd just called the police after the shooting happened."

"Maybe…maybe not," Kelsey said.

"According to Miami PD, you had an alibi for that day," Kyle stated. "Was it a lie?"

Kelsey nodded. "My mother lied to protect me. Savage had told her what happened. He told her that it was best that everyone says I'd been at home and never left the house."

"The police will want to talk to your mother," Phillipa said.

"She passed away this morning." Kelsey's voice broke again. "If she were still alive, I probably wouldn't have come here. I didn't want her to get into trouble."

"It's obvious you believe in protecting your family, Kelsey. But—"

She interrupted Phillipa by interjecting, "Please, no lectures…if I'd come forward sooner, Clara would still be alive. The way I see it, I killed her, too. And it's time for me to accept the consequences of my actions. I suppose I'll be held here until I'm returned to Miami." She sighed. "I told my husband everything and he's looking to hire an attorney to represent me." A lone tear escaped her eye. "I'm grateful he plans to stand by me."

Kelsey looked at Kyle. "You're Jon's brother, right?"

"I am," he responded.

"Please tell him that Clara really was a good person. She never wanted to harm anybody. She loved Myra like a sister. We both did."

Kyle gently replied, "Thank you for coming in and clearing this up for us."

After Kelsey was taken to be processed and placed into a holding cell, Phillipa said, "I'll call the detective at Miami PD."

"She was the final piece of the puzzle," he stated. "We finally have the whole story."

"I wish we'd been able to hear it from Helena's lips."

Kyle nodded in agreement. "All I can say is this has been nothing but a huge circle of deceit."

"At least we don't have to tell Jon that his wife murdered her friend," Phillipa responded.

"Thank goodness."

"I guess we should head over to the house," she said. "I'll call and tell Jon to expect us within the hour."

Kyle wasn't exactly looking forward to this conversation with his brother. He was thankful that Kelsey had chosen to come forward. At least Jon would never have to tell his children that their mother had murdered someone.

He checked in on his team before meeting Phillipa for the drive to Jon's house.

"Are you okay?" Phillipa asked when they were in the car.

"I keep thinking about the twins and what this is going to do to them," Kyle responded. "Jon will eventually accept what Paula did, but the girls… They looked to her as a surrogate mom."

She placed a hand on his arm. "They have your mother, Jon and you to help them through this."

"Yeah, they do, but there's nothing we can do to lessen the sting of betrayal they'll no doubt experience."

"Maybe Jon will consider counseling," Phillipa said.

"I'm going to suggest it." Kyle took her hand in his. "We'll all get through this somehow."

Phillipa smiled. "I know it. One thing I've learned about your family is that you're stronger together. It's what got you through the deaths of Helena and your father."

"They also got me through our breakup," he said.

"That's now a part of our past."

Kyle smiled. "Let's keep it back there."

"You won't get an argument from me," Phillipa responded.

His smile vanished when they turned into Jon's neighborhood. "I'm glad the girls are in school." He parked the car in the driveway. "I am not looking forward to this conversation."

"I know," Phillipa responded. "I'm not thrilled about it either."

He sighed, then said, "Let's get this over with."

"What's going on?" Jon asked when they entered the house. "Do you have any news on the case?"

"We do," Phillipa answered.

They settled in the living room to talk.

Amelie moved around the couch and sat down beside her oldest son. She took Jon's hand in her own. "Tell us…"

"We have a man in custody for the murder of Helena," Phillipa said. "And a woman… Paula."

"I knew it," Amelie uttered. "I had a feeling that manipulative woman had something to do with Helena's death."

"I can't believe it," Jon said. *"Paula. What was her part in my wife's murder?"*

"She conspired with a man named Miller Rowland to get rid of Helena. Paula wanted you for herself."

Amelie eyed Phillipa. "That's not the whole of it. What haven't you told us?"

She glanced over at Kyle. Phillipa didn't want to break Jon's heart, but he deserved to know the truth. She took a deep breath, then released it slowly. "Paula convinced Miller that Helena killed his sister."

Jon shook his head. "Noooo…there must be some mistake."

"There is more… Helena was born Clara Davis and she was from Miami—not Atlanta like she led you to believe." She paused then continued, "After her friend was killed, Helena left Miami and went to her father, who lived in Atlanta. He helped her create a new identity."

"I can't believe this," Jon repeated over and over. "My Helena was honest… She loved the Lord… She was a good person."

"Helena didn't shoot her friend," Phillipa announced. "Her cousin shot Myra Rowland to save Helena's life. Kelsey came to see me earlier. She told us everything."

Jon sat there shaking his head.

Amelie had been quiet until now. "Helena once asked me if I thought the good Lord really forgot all of our sins," she said. "I told her that He did…" Amelie looked over at Jon. "Son, I believe Helena tried to be the best person she could be. She loved you dearly and she loved those girls. Helena was young and scared. She made a mistake, but I believe she learned from it and spent the rest of her life trying to make amends. I saw the good in her."

"Helena didn't have anything to do with her friend's death," Kyle stated. "Myra Rowland was actually the aggressor."

Jon shook his head. "Then why did she run?"

"I believe she was scared," Kyle said.

"But you don't know for sure if she took part in her friend's murder, do you?"

"Actually, we do," Phillipa said. "Her cousin is the one who pulled the trigger in Myra Rowland's death. We're holding her until someone from Miami PD or the US Marshals transfers her back to Florida."

Jon let out a shaky sigh. "How did Paula connect with this man—the one who killed my wife?"

"Shortly before you and Helena got married, Paula found a degree and high school transcripts belonging to Clara Davis. She did some research and found the newspaper articles about Myra and Clara being missing. She contacted the Rowland family."

"So, all this time, Paula knew what happened but didn't say a word. I let that woman come around my children..." Jon's eyes glistened with a mixture of unshed tears and fiery anger. "What do I tell the girls? Paula is their godmother."

"Not anymore," Amelie interjected. "We won't let her have any more contact with the girls. I told Helena that she was making a mistake by doing that, but she kept saying Paula was her friend."

"We need to get back to the precinct," Phillipa said. "Jon, feel free to call me if you have questions or just need to talk. I'm sorry things turned out this way, but at least now you have answers."

Jon murmured a thank-you to both of them for delivering the news in person.

"One more thing," Phillipa said. "We will need your permission to conduct a DNA test on Helena's remains to prove that she is really Clara Davis."

He nodded. "Send me the necessary paperwork."

"I feel horrible," she whispered when they got to the car. "Jon is devastated."

"He's in shock right now. I'm going to stay with him for a little while," Kyle said.

"That's a great idea. But first, if you're not busy later tonight, can you come by the house?" she asked. "I'd like to talk to you."

"Sure."

When Phillipa returned to the precinct, she took a deep intake of breath and exhaled slowly. She was glad that part was over. It was never easy making notifications or updates on cases like this.

She sat down at her desk to finalize the complete investigation summary of Helena's case. Phillipa schedule a meeting with the assigned prosecutor to turn over the murder book and respond to any additional questions that may come up during the preparation for the Grand Jury.

At the end of the workday, Phillipa checked to see if Kyle was in his office. She found him at his desk staring at the computer monitor.

Phillipa knocked softly on the open door. "Hey, I thought you were going to call it a day."

He gave her a tiny smile. "I thought about it but changed my mind. It's better if I keep busy."

"Are you planning to be here much longer?"

"For another hour," Kyle responded. "Are you heading out?"

"I am."

"If you're not too tired, would you mind still coming to the house later?" Phillipa asked. "My timing probably sucks but I'm hoping we can talk. I'd rather not put it off any longer."

"Is it okay if I come around seven-thirty?"

"Yes, that's perfect. I'll see you then."

Phillipa hoped that the conversation later would lift Kyle's spirits some. The shadows across her heart had dissipated. She was finally ready to admit her feelings to him. She'd always known that Kyle was the only man for her.

But she had one more thing to do before she talked to him. Sitting in the SUV, Phillipa pulled out her cell phone.

When the person on the other end answered, she said, "Gary, it's me. Are you busy?"

"Is everything okay?" he asked. "Is something wrong with Raya?"

"No, she's fine. There's nothing wrong," she assured him. "I just wanted to talk to you."

There was a slight pause before he asked, "About what?"

"First, I wanted to say congratulations on your upcoming marriage. I'm very happy for you."

"Thank you," he said, "but I'm sure that's not the real reason for this call."

"No, it isn't," Phillipa said. She paused a heartbeat before saying, "Gary, I'm calling because I want to say that I'm really sorry for the hurt I caused you. You were a good husband and father. You certainly deserved better than what I gave you."

"I know you didn't set out to intentionally hurt me. I should've realized that you hadn't gotten over your own heartbreak. I guess I just thought my love could heal you, and I was wrong."

"We were both wrong," Phillipa said. "I thought the same thing."

"Have you seen him?"

"Yes."

"Have you picked up where you left off?"

"Not really. We're starting from scratch, so to speak."

"How is Raya doing?"

"She's adjusting well." Phillipa hesitated as she searched for the right words, then said, "She had been hoping we'd get back together. That's why she was so upset. She also worried that you won't be the same after you get married."

He sighed. "She and Francine were getting along well until I told her about the engagement."

"Maybe it's out of some fierce loyalty to me. I explained that Francine will be one more person to love her."

"How is she dealing with you seeing someone?"

"I think she's adjusting now that she knows you and I won't ever get back together. Gary, would you consider coming to Charlotte? You and Francine?"

"Sure, if you think it would help."

"I think if we present a united front, Raya will feel better about your marriage and my relationship with Kyle. She likes him, but if things between him and I progress… I'm not sure how she'll respond."

"We'll fly in this weekend."

"Great," Phillipa said. "See you then."

She released a sigh of contentment. She'd found a

way to lay the past to rest. Now it was time for her to look toward the future—a future with Kyle.

Kyle wasn't sure what to expect, but he chose to remain hopeful that night as he pulled up to Phillipa's parents' house. He got out of the car and walked to the front door.

Phillipa opened it and stepped aside. "Thanks for coming."

They sat down in the living room.

"The reason I wanted to speak with you is because I need to apologize."

"For what?" Kyle asked with a frown.

"I was wrong to blame you for the breakdown of my marriage. I never should've gotten married when I knew I wasn't over you. It wasn't fair to Gary. When things started to go south—it was just easier to blame you. I didn't want to accept my part in any of this. Seeing Miller and all that anger... I realized that I was just like him—walking around sowing seeds of anger and refusing to forgive. Kyle, I'm so sorry."

"There are so many things I wished I'd done differently—like go out to California to convince you to marry me."

"You once asked me if I still had any feelings for you... The answer is yes. Kyle, I never once stopped loving you. Don't get me wrong—I didn't want to love you. I fought it with every fiber of my being."

"Same here," he responded with a chuckle.

"I hope you can forgive me."

Pulling her close to him, Kyle whispered, "Yes, I can."

* * * * *